THE VENOMOUS ECLIPSE

by Adrianne Ambrose

Penguin Young Readers Licenses
An Imprint of Penguin Random House

D1012035

PENGUIN YOUNG READERS LICENSES
An Imprint of Penguin Random House LLC

Cover illustration by Dan Panosian.

ISBN 9780515159707

10 9 8 7 6 5 4 3 2 1

Chapter 1

It was a beautiful day in Angel Grove with scarcely a cloud in the sky. Jason Scott and Zack Taylor were over at Billy Cranston's house, hanging out in his garage. It wouldn't have been so bad if they could have opened the garage door, but there was no way that was going to happen. Billy was working on so many cutting-edge inventions that leaving the door open would draw the attention of people walking past. Plus, a lot of the inventions would reveal the guys' secret identities as members of the Power Rangers, so the door definitely had to stay shut.

"Hey, Billy. How's it going?" Zack asked. "Are you almost done? We're burning daylight." So much pent-up energy flowed through the Black Ranger's body that he was bouncing on his toes, practically vibrating with the need to get out of the garage and into the sunshine.

"Almost done," Billy said, pulling a bandana out of a pocket of his blue overalls to polish his glasses. Even though he was a scientific genius, the Blue Ranger still favored blue overalls above any other article of clothing. "I need a few more minutes. Just want to make sure Jason's wrist communicator is functioning properly."

"Yeah, you want my wrist communicator to work, don't you?" Jason said with an amused grin, looking up from his workout. As the Red Ranger and the leader of the Power Rangers, he liked to keep busy, so he'd unearthed some dust-covered free weights in the corner of the garage and was currently exercising his biceps.

The Power Rangers' wrist communicators looked just like ordinary fitness watches to the outside world, but they were actually how the Rangers communicated with Zordon and Alpha 5 at the Command Center. They also kept the Rangers in touch with one another during an emergency. Plus, when necessary, their space-age wrist devices enabled the Power Rangers to teleport to the Command Center, or wherever else they needed to go. A malfunctioning communicator could mean the difference between victory and defeat.

"Sure," Zack said. "If it worked, that'd be helpful." He then did a cool slide across the garage floor and finished the move by adding a roundhouse kick and a double-fist punch. Zack loved dancing almost as much as he loved being a Power Ranger. In fact, he frequently incorporated dance moves into his fighting style, even developing his own dance-based martial art called Hip Hop Kido. He'd also taught a couple classes in it at the Angel Grove Youth Center.

"Zack, watch out for my orange banana," Billy exclaimed, jumping to his feet and hurrying over to a workbench close to where the Black Ranger was dancing.

"Your orange banana?!" both Jason and Zack exclaimed at the same time, exchanging amazed looks.

"Let's see it," said Jason.

"Let's eat it," added Zack.

"It's not really an orange banana," the Blue Ranger explained a little apologetically. He didn't enjoy disappointing his friends. "That's just what I call my organic molecular rearranger laser."

"Your what-uh what-uh what-uh laser?" asked Zack.

"It's just a laser that rearranges the molecular structure of organic matter," Billy told them. "At least, that's what it's supposed to do." He then frowned, knitting his eyebrows together as he thought about the challenges he was facing with the invention.

"Billy," Jason said, "you realize we don't have Trini here to translate your science speak. Can you explain it again, but this time in English?"

"Okay, fine." Billy was used to his friends not always following his train of thought when he was talking about science. "Let's say you have an orange, but you don't want an orange. You want a banana. I'm working on a laser that can change molecular structure. So basically a laser that can turn an orange into a banana."

"An orange banana," both Jason and Zack said, nodding their heads and laughing. Leave it to the Blue Ranger to come up with an idea like that.

"So, let's see it work," Zack said eagerly. He loved getting to use Billy's inventions; especially if it was something that could help fight Rita and her flunkies. But inventions involving food were also interesting.

"Well . . ." Billy looked a little glum. "That's the problem," he told them. "It's doesn't work. Not really."

"Come on," Zack said, his hand poised to press a button on the device. "Just one little demo."

"Don't touch," Billy said. "Please," he added. "It's just . . . it's in a fragile state because it's not in its metal housing. Anyway, I'm out of fruit."

"Hold up," Jason said, coming over to stand by his friends. "Billy's the scientist and he says it's not ready, so I think we have to respect that. And besides," he added, "it's his toy; he calls the shots."

"Otherwise he might take his laser and go home," Zack said with a laugh. And then he turned to the Blue Ranger. "Sorry, Billy. It's just you make a lot of cool stuff, and sometimes it's really tempting to push a button or two."

"That's all right," Billy told him. "But it's best to be familiar with a machine's capabilities before you use it."

"That's right," Zack added. "What if your laser ended up turning an orange into a lima bean? That would be a complete waste of good fruit."

Billy went back to where he was fixing the wrist communicator. "Okay," he said, handing the watch to the Red Ranger, "why don't you give this a quick test and then we should be all set to go."

"Sounds good," said Zack. "Kimberly and Trini are probably already at the beach."

Jason strapped on the communicator and then pressed the transmit button. "Alpha 5. Come in, Alpha 5," he said.

"This is Alpha 5," said the mechanical-sounding voice belonging to the robot, Alpha 5. He basically ran everything at the Command Center because Zordon, an alien and the Power Rangers' mentor, still struggled to escape a time warp that held him trapped between two dimensions. "Hello, Red Ranger. It's good to hear from you. How may I assist?"

"Sorry to bother you, Alpha. I was just testing to see if my wrist communicator was working again," Jason admitted.

"You're coming in loud and clear," the robot told him. "Is there anything else you wish to communicate?"

"Not really," Jason said. "We're about to hit the beach."

"Have a pleasant afternoon," the robot told him.

"Roger that." The Red Ranger grinned at his friends before saying, "Surf's up."

Chapter 2

Meanwhile, in Rita Repulsa's fortress on the moon, the sorceress was in her usual foul mood. "Where are those blasted Power Rangers?" she demanded, stomping around her observatory, her long brown-and-gold robes swishing behind her. She tucked a white lock of hair into her elaborate two-peaked headdress and peered through her telescope at the little corner of Earth known as Angel Grove. "I need to get rid of Zordon's nasty little pets so that I can finally conquer Earth!"

"Yes, oh mighty sorceress," agreed Baboo. "That is an excellent plan."

"But how?" she demanded, taking a swat at the creature that looked like his father was a monkey and his mother was a bat. "I need a new plan. Those disgusting do-gooders keep defeating every monster I throw at them."

There was the sound of a bell chiming, and a few moments later a second minion, Squatt, came stumbling into the room. He was out of breath and obviously excited. "Your royal . . . most excellent . . . Rita," he gasped. "I . . . we . . . she . . ." He was wheezing so heavily that he couldn't get out any words.

"What is it, you blithering buffoon? I don't have all day," Rita screeched.

"She's here," Squatt managed to say after taking a deep breath. He was so excited that his blue skin was sweating. While dabbing at his enormous goblin chin with a cloth, he continued with, "Your guest, Scorpina, has finally arrived."

"Well, why didn't you say something sooner?" Rita demanded. "Don't just stand there sweating like a toad. Where is she? Lead her in!" she said, giving him a shove. "Get some refreshments."

Even though Squatt started rushing back toward the door, it was too late for him to properly escort Rita's guest into the observatory. Scorpina had already shown herself the way.

Scorpina appeared to be her usual, charming self. Her gold scorpion-shell armor was polished to a high shine and clung snugly to her body.

"Darling Rita," Scorpina said, tilting her head and smiling while she looked out of the corner of her eye. "Would you have me wait in the entrance hall all day?"

"Scorpina, old friend!" Rita exclaimed.

"Not too old I hope," Scorpina said with a laugh, running a hand over her gold, shell-like helmet.

"No, not old at all," Baboo hurried to say.

"Neither one of you looks a day over four hundred," Squatt felt the need to add.

"Shush," Baboo hissed at his friend, giving him an elbow. "Leave the compliments to me."

"So, why have you summoned me?" Scorpina asked, strutting across the room to the telescope. "Still trying to get rid of those awful Power Rangers so you can conquer this puny blue planet? What's it called again?" She took a moment to think it over. "Oh, yes . . . Earth."

"Can't I just want to spend some time with my friend?" Rita asked with a hand to her heart, pretending to be hurt.

"You could," was the lady scorpion's amused reply, "but I wouldn't believe you."

"You hurt my feelings," Rita insisted. "And here I had Baboo make you such a pretty present."

Upon hearing this, Scorpina lit up with excitement, a big smile spreading her ruby red lips. "A present? For me?"

Spinning around to glare at Baboo, Rita said, "What are you waiting for? Go get it."

"Yes, your royal evilness," Baboo said with a hasty bow, before scampering from the room.

Rita rubbed her forehead, as if trying to fight off a headache. "It's so hard to get good help these days."

"So tell me," Scorpina said while they were waiting, "is Zordon really giving you that much trouble?"

"Zordon," the sorceress said with disgust. "I'd probably be rid of him already if it weren't for those horrid, helmet-headed freaks. It's the Power Rangers. They always ruin all my beautifully wicked plans."

Just then Baboo hurried back into the room holding a small, wrapped box in his hands. "I have it, Your Majesty," he called.

"Let me see it!" Squatt squealed, rushing toward his friend.

"No," said Baboo, holding the box in the air to keep

it out of the shorter minion's reach. "It's for Scorpina."

"Oh, come on," Squatt said, jumping up and down while trying to grab the box. "Just give me a little peek."

"Get out of the way, you nitwits," Rita yelled, snatching the box from Baboo. "Stand back. You keep clowning around like that and you're going to knock somebody over." Then, sweeping across the room, she approached her friend with the small trinket box extended on the palm of her hand. "This is for you," she said. "I had Baboo make it especially for you."

Chapter 3

"What is it?" Scorpina asked, eagerly tearing off the colorful paper and flipping open the lid.

Inside the box was a gold ring with a round, glowing yellow jewel on the top. "Rita, you didn't!" Scorpina exclaimed.

"I did," was the sorceress's reply, a wicked grin on her face. "It's an Eclipse Ring. I had Baboo make it exactly like the ring you lost when we were conquering the Zelton Galaxy. Or was it the Xelton Galaxy?"

"Zelton," Scorpina said decisively.

Rita waved a dismissive hand through the air. "Oh, who can remember?"

Scorpina pulled the ring out of the box and slipped it on her finger. Extending her hand to admire the ring, she said, "It's absolutely lovely. Does it work like my old one?"

Baboo rushed forward to answer. "It should, your

scorpion-ness. I made it to Rita's exact specifications."

"Let's give it a little test run," Scorpina said, pointing her new ring in Squatt's direction.

"Eek!" shrieked the blue warthog-like creature, dashing across the room as fast as he could run before she could get him in her sights.

"Maybe leave my minions alone," Rita suggested to her guest. "At least until I can find some more suitable replacements."

"Okay, fine," Scorpina said with a cruel laugh. She adjusted her aim, choosing to point the ring at Rita's telescope. Then she lifted a well-concealed latch on the ring and twisted the yellow stone in the center. A bright beam of golden light shot out of the ring and surrounded the telescope. The instrument glowed for a moment and then vanished. When Scorpina closed the latch and lowered her arm, the formerly brilliant yellow stone was now black as faceted obsidian.

"Where'd it go?" Squatt yelled, running over to where the telescope had stood just moments earlier. "What happened to the telescope?" He began swiping his hands through the air.

"Don't do that. You might knock it over, you

nincompoop!" Rita bellowed.

"But, Your Majesty, it's gone," the minion insisted.

"It is and it isn't," she said with a shrug. "It's gone, but not completely. It's an Eclipse Ring."

"Oh, an Eclipse Ring," Squatt said, nodding his head, although it was obvious he was still confused.

Baboo pulled his friend aside. "You know what happens with a solar eclipse, right?"

"Yes," said Squatt, but then he quickly followed that up with, "No."

"A solar eclipse is when the moon passes between Earth and the sun, making it look like the sun has disappeared. It hasn't, really. People on Earth just can't see the sun because the moon is in the way."

"Oh." Squatt scratched his head. "So Rita's telescope is still there, only we can't see it because the moon is in the way?"

"Not exactly." Baboo shook his head. "With the Eclipse Ring, the telescope is still there, but just in an alternate dimension."

Squatt reached out and felt around in the air close to where the telescope had just been standing. "So it's invisible?"

"No," Baboo went on. "It's still there, just not in this dimension. It's like it's in the dimension next door."

"Wow." Squatt's eyes grew round as he tried to take it all in.

"There's something I forgot to tell you," Baboo said, turning back to Rita and her guest. "I know you didn't request it, Your Majesty, but I took the liberty of making one tiny modification of my own to the ring."

Rita's eyes narrowed. "Took it upon yourself, did you?" she growled. "Well, this had better be good."

"I hope you'll approve," Baboo said, obviously feeling nervous about making changes to the ring without getting his leader's approval. "I made it so that Scorpina doesn't have to bring an object back before she can make another object disappear. Now it's a rapid-fire Eclipse Ring rather than just a single shot. She should be able to easily blast all of the Power Rangers into an alternate dimension, even if she ends up doing it one Ranger at a time."

"Ha-ha-ha!" Rita released howls of laughter. "So all Scorpina has to do is keep blasting until the Power Rangers are all gone? I'll be rid of those annoying teenagers forever? That's brilliant!"

"Thank you, your evilness," Baboo said, sounding both flattered and relieved.

Scorpina grinned, admiring the ring even more. "Now that's what I call an upgrade."

"I'm glad you're pleased with your present," Rita said to her friend. "But I am going to need my telescope back, you know. So if you wouldn't mind . . ." She waved her hand at the empty space where the instrument used to be.

"Of course," Scorpina said, raising her hand. She depressed a well-concealed button on the side of the ring and gave the top a twist in the opposite direction. Another beam of light came shooting out of the ring, this one dark like a shadow. At first only a silhouette of the telescope appeared. And then, half a second later, the whole thing was back, exactly like it was before. The ring's stone now appeared canary yellow once more.

"Hooray!" Squatt shouted, clapping and jumping up and down. "I love magic!"

"I love this gift," Scorpina said. "And here I didn't get you anything."

"Oh, that's okay," Rita told her. "But if you're feeling like you want to return the favor, you could always go down to Earth and cause a little trouble for the Power Rangers." After which she added, "I mean, only if you feel like getting some exercise."

This made Scorpina laugh. "Rita, you'll never change. But I love my present and I'd be happy to get rid of the Power Rangers for you, once and for all. Should I dispose of Zordon, as well, and his annoying little robot friend? Or would you like to do that yourself?"

"Get rid of them all!" Rita practically shouted. "I'm sick of trying to conquer this puny planet. With the Power Rangers and Zordon out of the way, I can crush Earth under my boot heel and then move on to conquering something more interesting."

"You'll be in a new part of the galaxy by next week," Baboo said.

"She will if I have anything to say about it," Scorpina said with a laugh.

"Take Baboo with you. And a platoon of Putty Patrollers, if you want," Rita offered.

"Why not?" Scorpina shrugged. "Come on, Baboon."

"Begging your pardon, Miss Scorpina, but it's Baboo," the vampire monkey corrected her, although he did it rather meekly.

"Baboo, Baboon, whatever," Scorpina said with a wave of her hand. "As long as you follow orders, then I don't care what you call yourself." She ran a hand over her gold helmet and then adjusted some of the plates that formed the iron claw of her left hand. "Now let's teleport down to Angel Grove and get the job done."

"Don't forget about me," Squatt called, rushing over to teleport with them. "I want to play with the ring, too."

But the blue warthog wasn't nearly as coordinated as he believed himself to be. He ended up crashing into Scorpina and Baboo just as they were starting to teleport and knocking them over. Two seconds later, the three of them tumbled onto the beach just outside of Angel Grove.

"You idiot!" Scorpina shouted, trying to push the blue goon off of her. "I should send you to an alternate dimension for that." Then she looked down and noticed that her hand was bare. "My ring!" she cried. "It's gone!"

"It must have fallen off your finger while we were leaving Rita's fortress," Baboo said, getting up and dusting the sand from his clothes.

"Rita will kill me if she thinks I've lost it," Scorpina said, getting to her feet. "I must go back for it."

"We'll go with you," Baboo offered.

"No," Scorpina snapped. "You stay here with the blueberry warthog and wait for the Putty Patrollers to arrive. They should be here any second. Stay out of sight, and I'll be back in a moment." With that, she was gone.

"I think I hear voices," Squatt said after they'd been standing on the beach for a good ten seconds.

"Sounds like humans," Baboo said, hearing the voices, too. "Quick, behind that bluff before anybody sees us."

Chapter 4

By the time the boys got to the beach, Trini Kwan and Kimberly Hart had already set up the volleyball net, laid out beach towels, and inflated a couple of rafts.

"Hey," Kimberly called when she spotted Jason, Zack, and Billy approaching. "You found us." She was wearing pink shorts, a pink bikini top, and pink flip-flops. It was her favorite color, and just happened to be her Ranger color.

"I hope you remembered lunch," Trini added, smiling at the guys. "We're starving." She had on yellow-and-white-striped shorts and a pale yellow tank top. Her long, glossy black hair made a striking contrast with her Ranger color.

"Sandwiches, drinks, music, sunscreen—we brought everything," Zack said with a broad smile as the guys toted a few bags across the short spit of beach that created Angel Grove Cove.

Most people stuck to the main beach because it was easier to access, but the Power Rangers preferred the smaller beach that was surrounded by bluffs. That way they didn't draw any attention if they got a call from Zordon on their wrist communicators or suddenly had to morph. Plus, with no one else around, they could show off, using their awesome superhero acrobatics while playing their own special version of volleyball.

"Who's up for a game of power volley?" Trini asked, picking a side of the volleyball net. Tossing the volleyball up into the air, she raised her arm and brought it down hard, firing the ball over the net.

Power volley had similar rules to volleyball, but with martial arts moves and Ranger strength.

The boys set down their gear and peeled off their shirts.

"I'm in," Zack said, scooping up the ball and grabbing a position in the sand on the other side of the net from Trini.

"Me too," said Kimberly, joining Zack on his side of the net.

"I'm with Trini and her killer serve," said Jason,

aligning himself with the Yellow Ranger.

"How about you, Billy?" Kimberly called. "Are you ready for a little friendly competition?"

"Maybe later," the Blue Ranger told her. "Right now I want to set up Zack's radio to run on solar power. That way we won't have to delay if we run out of batteries and need to grab more," he said, pushing his glasses back up to the bridge of his nose.

Jason smiled. "Leave it to Billy to come to the beach and then work on a science project."

"Fine by me," said Zack, tossing the ball into the air a few times to warm up. "I'm all for free tunes." He turned his attention to the game. "All right, team Jini," he said, combining his two opponents' names. "Prepare to lose."

Jason laughed. "Go ahead, Zimberly. You can try."

Then Zack threw the ball very high, straight up in the air. Quick as lightning, he did a jump-spin crescent kick, and then hammered the ball across the net for his opening serve.

Jason dove for it, but was unable to stop the ball. "That's Zimberly one, Jini zero," the Black Ranger said, high-fiving his teammate.

But Trini managed to block Zack's next serve, setting up Jason to spike the ball over the net.

"Good try, but now it's Jini's serve," Jason said, enjoying the friendly rivalry. "Here comes the hammer." He tossed the ball to Trini and said, "Give them a taste of your killer serve."

"You got it," Trini said. "Just feed me the ball. I'm going to take a spin."

"Okay," said Jason.

Trini backed up. As soon as the Red Ranger tossed the ball into the air, Trini started twirling across the sand.

Then, as the ball dropped within range, she kicked one foot into the air and quickly followed it with the other, so that her body was practically parallel with the ground as she came into contact with the ball, which went rocketing over the net.

"Got it!" Zack called, and he tried his hardest to save the point, diving onto the sand. But the ball was going too fast and it bounced just out of his reach.

Jason raised his hand above his head to high-five the Yellow Ranger. "Awesome butterfly kick," he said.

"You okay over there?" Trini called when Zack

didn't immediately pop back up on his feet to keep playing.

"Yeah, I'm okay," Zack said. "It's just, I found something."

"What is it?" Kimberly asked, walking over to where he was sitting on the sand.

"Some kind of fancy ring," the Black Ranger said, extending the bauble toward her. "Check out that yellow stone. It's so bright; I've never seen anything like it."

"It must be a topaz," Kimberly said, moving the ring a little so the stone could catch the sun.

"I thought a topaz was blue," Trini said. She and Jason had crossed the net to have a closer look at Zack's discovery.

"They can come in blue, pink, orange, yellow; lots of different colors," Kimberly said. "But this stone is unusual. It's much brighter than anything I've ever seen."

"Well, then keep it," Zack said affably. "I mean, I'm not going to wear it."

"No, I can't," Kimberly said. "I'm sure whoever lost this ring wants it back. Besides, the stone is so bright, I think there's a chance it might be a canary diamond."

"A diamond of that size and color would be very unusual," Billy said, being lured away from the radio by the discovery.

"Then we should try to find the owner," Trini said.

Zack shrugged. "Sure, but how? We can't exactly go around saying, 'Hey, did you lose a really expensive ring?' or anything like that. We don't want it to end up with the wrong person."

"We could put up flyers," Kimberly replied. "But not give the ring's description."

"Or maybe even swing by the police department to see if anyone reported the ring missing," Jason suggested.

"May I see the ring?" Billy asked. Kimberly handed it to him. "Hmm," he said, taking off his glasses and squinting at the trinket. "This is a very complex mounting and seems to have some type of mechanical element."

"A mechanical ring?" Trini couldn't help but raise her dark eyebrows. "What does it do?"

"I'm not sure," Billy told her, handing the ring back to Zack. "But if we can't find the owner, I'd like to take a closer look."

Chapter 5

Meanwhile, behind the bluffs above the cove, Baboo, Squatt, and a platoon of Putties were watching the teens.

"I think they've found Scorpina's ring," Squatt said.

Baboo adjusted his monocle. "I believe you're right."

"We should try to get it back from them," Squatt went on. "Then maybe Scorpina will be nice to us."

"I don't think she'll be nice," Baboo told him, "but maybe she'll be less scary. I still tremble whenever I think about the last time she battled the Power Rangers. I can't believe they survived."

"Me too," said Squatt. "But how are we going to get that ring back?"

"I have an idea," said Rita's monkey minion. "But it's not for me or you to do. Grab one of the Putties."

Back on the beach, the Power Rangers were

sitting down for some lunch. "I know looking for the owner of a lost ring won't exactly be death-defying, but I still want to fuel up before we do anything else," Jason said. "And then maybe finish our game before we head out."

"Oh, look," said Zack, squinting at the bluffs. "Here comes an elderly woman, headed right this way. Maybe she lost the ring?" Everyone looked up to get a peek at the new arrival.

"Getting to the cove is quite a hike, especially for a senior citizen," Jason observed. "She must be in amazing shape."

"That's kind of a funny outfit to wear to the beach," Billy commented. "Do older women usually wear jeans under a sundress?"

"Not with a knit shawl on top," Trini told him. "But look at that hat. It's so big; maybe she's just trying to stay out of the sun."

"Guys," Kimberly said, rising to her knees and staring harder at the approaching figure. "I don't think that's a woman. Call me crazy, but I think that might be a Putty."

"What's a Putty doing here?" Billy asked.

Everybody sprang to their feet.

Putties appeared from every crest of the bluffs. "Let's get moving, team," the Red Ranger said. "We're surrounded."

Chapter 6

A swarm of Putties came charging down from the bluffs. They immediately had the Power Rangers surrounded on three sides.

Glancing over his shoulder, Jason saw that behind them there was nothing but ocean. The teens were either going to have to fight their way out of the cove or swim for Hawaii.

As usual, the Putties were completely gray—except for the one that was wearing the old-lady disguise.

"Why are they attacking us?" Kimberly wanted to know. It seemed very random for just a sunny afternoon at the cove.

"I don't know," Jason said. "Maybe they wanted to use this part of the beach."

"They could have just asked," Zack added. "We would have shared."

The air was filled with the strange little burbling

noises the Putties always made. The Power Rangers assumed it was their way of communicating with one another, but it made no sense to human ears.

"Should we morph?" the Pink Ranger asked as the Putties got closer.

"No," Jason told her. "It's just a bunch of Putties. It'll be good to practice without the Ranger Powers."

"You got it," said Zack, taking a crane stance, balancing on one leg, with the other leg bent and resting on his knee. He was ready to kick any Putty within leg's reach.

"No problem," said Billy, assuming a back stance, his weight on the leg he had positioned behind him so that he was prepared to kick or punch.

"We're with you," agreed Kimberly, striking an hourglass stance, her weight distributed so she could move forward or backward quickly and with equal ease.

"Let's do this," Trini said, posing in a cat foot stance with one foot poised in front of her, ready to strike.

The Power Rangers had all assumed a defensive position as the Putties initiated their assault. "Come on, team," Jason said from his power stance. "Let's show these Putties that picking a fight with the Power Rangers is no day at the beach."

"*Hi-yah!*" Trini said, launching into the air and executing a fierce flying front kick that sent a Putty staggering.

"*Yah!*" shouted Jason, taking out two Putties with a spinning split kick.

A Putty came at Kimberly and she did a quick aerial, deploying her gymnastics skills to avoid the creature. Then she took the Putty down with a well-placed spinning back kick and a palm-fist strike.

"Eat sand, Putty Patroller!" she said, coiling her body into a tiger stance in anticipation of the next attack.

Three Putties were coming at Jason, but the Red Ranger wasn't worried. He snatched up one of the beach towels and taunted the Putties with it like a matador waving a cape.

"Toro, toro, toro," Jason said, just like the bullfighters do in Spain. His attackers fell for it and they were quickly staggering from a series of blows.

Concerned that he might lose the ring, Zack stuck

it on his finger as the Putties were closing in. But he was quickly confronted by six Putties, so all thoughts of looking out for someone else's property were driven out of his head.

The Black Ranger always loved incorporating dance moves into his fighting whenever he could, so he did a quick step spin to distract his assailants. It worked—the Putties were confused and mesmerized—but Zack didn't notice that he'd also accidentally bumped the latch on the ring.

By the time the spin was over, there were only two Putties trying to fight him.

"Hey, weren't there a few more of you a moment ago?" Zack asked with a frown. The Putties only burbled as they came charging at him. Zack was confused, but decided not to look a gift horse in the mouth. He quickly dispatched the duo by grabbing the first one by the arm and flipping it at the second.

With his opponents temporarily out of commission, Zack scanned the area to see if any other members of the team needed help. They appeared to all be holding their own. The ring was a tight fit, and he twisted at it, trying to give his finger underneath some circulation. When he looked back at the Putties he'd been fighting just seconds earlier, they were gone.

"W-what?" the Black Ranger stammered, scratching his head. Were his eyes playing tricks on him? But there was no time to puzzle over the mystery because Billy was quickly being overwhelmed by several Putties.

"Hey, Zack," Billy called as one of the Putties lunged for the radio. "I think they like your music."

"Why are they going after that?" Zack wondered aloud. It was just a cheap radio, after all. The best thing about it was Billy's modifications.

"I don't know," the Blue Ranger told him. "Maybe they're interested in solar power. Why don't you come over here and help me figure it out."

Billy leaped into the air, executing a split kick that knocked two of the Putties to the ground. "Find your own tunes," he told them.

But then another Putty grabbed the radio, looked underneath it, shook it, and then threw it on the ground. Zack frowned. "I guess they're not trying to steal my tunes, after all."

"But what are they doing here?" asked Trini as she did a knife hands block and then struck back at her opponent. "They're not here just to catch some waves."

"Maybe those two know," Jason said, indicating the top of the bluffs, where Baboo and Squatt were watching the action, safe out of harm's way, as usual.

"I think maybe we should ask them," Zack said, spinning a Putty around and then sweeping its legs out from underneath it with a heel hook.

Kimberly did a series of handsprings to avoid the Putty trying to grab her, but then the creature snatched up a beach towel and shook it, instead. "Come on," Kimberly said. "Let's go find out why the flying monkey and the blueberry warthog are here."

"Yeah," said Zack.

"We're on it," Trini agreed.

"Let's go!" Jason said after dispatching another Putty with a brutal elbow slam.

The Power Rangers raced across the sand, leaving the Putties in their wake. They all knew that if Baboo and Squatt were there, it definitely meant something sinister was about to happen.

Up on the bluffs, Squatt was becoming alarmed. "Uh, Baboo? I think they see us."

"They can't possibly," Baboo said, brushing some sand off of his monocle. "We're too far away, and they're battling too many Putties."

"Okay, if you say so," was his blue friend's reply, "but—"

"Why would you even think such a thing?" Baboo asked, fitting his monocle back over his eye.

Squatt scratched his head. "Um, I don't know, probably because they're running right for us."

"Gah!" Springing to his feet, Baboo shouted, "Why didn't you say something?"

This confused Squatt. "I thought I did."

"We have to get out of here!" Baboo wailed.

"But we don't have the . . . uh . . . thingy that the scorpion lady lost," Squatt pointed out.

"Scorpina probably found the Eclipse Ring back on the moon," Baboo insisted as he started to run.

"Oh." The blue warthog scratched his head some more. "Does that even make sense? I mean, didn't we see the Black Ranger find it?"

"Don't talk to me about sense," his friend shouted over his shoulder as he hotfooted it out of there. "We don't have time for sense. We'll make up a better excuse when we get back to the moon!"

Chapter 7

"Where'd they go?" Kimberly asked, scanning the landscape when they reached the top of the bluffs. "They were just here a minute ago." But the bluffs were bare; Rita's two henchmen were gone.

"They must have teleported when we weren't looking," Billy told her. "I thought maybe I saw a flash while we were climbing." He turned to glance over his shoulder, back at the small beach. "The Putty Patrollers are gone, too."

"There's no way Putties could get out of the cove that quickly on foot," Jason said, looking over the sand as well. "Everyone must be back on the moon with Rita."

"Yeah, maybe a couple of the Putties teleported during the fight," Zack said. "It seemed kind of strange at the time, but Rita must have pulled them out of here for some reason. I wonder what she's up to?"

Trini shrugged, flipping her long hair over her shoulder. "I'm sure whatever it is, she's up to no good, as usual."

"We need to update Zordon and Alpha," Jason said, pressing a button on his wrist communicator. "Come in, Alpha 5," he said, speaking into the device.

A robotic voice quickly replied, "Hello, Jason. What's happening? I thought you and the other Power Rangers were spending your afternoon at the beach."

"We were," Jason said, keeping his voice low, even though nobody else was around besides his fellow teammates. "But then Baboo and Squatt decided to crash the party, along with dozens of Putty Patrollers."

"Aye-yi-yi," the robot said, and the Rangers knew that he probably had both his hands pressed against his big metal head. "Is everyone okay?"

"We're fine," Jason assured him. "They just interrupted a good game of power volley, that's all."

"What was their objective?" Alpha 5 wanted to know.

"We're not sure," Jason replied. "We chased after them, but they must have teleported back to the moon. Will you and Zordon see if you can find out the reason for their surprise visit?"

"Anything for you and the team, Jason. We'll see what we can find out," the robot said.

"Thanks, Alpha," the Red Ranger said with a smile. "Power Rangers out." And then he ended the communication.

"So what do we do now?" Billy asked. Their fun day at the beach hadn't turned out to be much fun; their lunch was covered in sand, the rafts were deflated, and the volleyball net was in a giant tangle thanks to the Putty Patrollers.

"Let's pack up our gear and go get some milk shakes at the Youth Center," Jason suggested as a way to try to salvage the day. "Zordon and Alpha 5 will let us know if we have anything to worry about from Rita."

"We probably do," Trini said. "I doubt Baboo and Squatt would have come to the beach on their own just to catch some rays."

"But milk shakes sound like a good way to pass the time while we're waiting to find out Rita's next evil plan," Zack added. And then he looked down at his hand. "Oh, and we can try to figure out who lost this ring."

"Good idea," Kimberly agreed as the Power

Rangers headed back down the bluff to pack up their beach gear. "It's such an old-fashioned style; I bet it's an heirloom or something."

Twenty minutes later and the friends were grabbing a table at the Youth Center. "I'll order the shakes," Jason said, before heading over to chat with Ernie at the counter.

"I'm still wondering what was going on with those Putties," Zack said as he flipped his chair backward and then straddled it. "I've never known Rita to teleport Putty Patrollers during a fight. I mean, why would she suddenly care about them?"

"I don't know," Billy said, rubbing his chin. "Do you think she did teleport them?"

Zack shook his head and shrugged. "I'm not sure," he admitted. "It was weird. They were there one minute, and then they were gone. It was like they'd vanished."

"Curious," said Billy. "I wonder what happened to them."

"I'm going to get started making the flyer for the ring," Kimberly said.

"I'll help you," Trini said, getting to her feet. "I

know Ernie has some paper and markers behind the counter." She raised her voice a little to call to the manager of the Youth Center. "Ernie, can we borrow some of your paper and markers? We need to make a flyer for a ring we found."

"Sure, go ahead, kids," Ernie said affably. He really liked Trini and her friends. "Help yourself to whatever you need."

Chapter 8

Across the room Skull elbowed Bulk and nodded toward Trini and Kimberly.

"What are they up to?" he asked in a low voice. Skull was skinny with greasy hair and an oily personality to match.

"Guess we better find out," was Bulk's reply as he hauled his immense frame out of his chair.

"What's this?" Skull said, snatching up the flyer that Kimberly and Trini were starting to block out. He squinted at the words, trying to make them out. "Found: Gold ring."

"Is this it?" Bulk asked, grabbing the ring with the yellow stone before Kimberly could stop him.

"Give that back," Kimberly demanded. "And mind your own business."

"But this is my business," Bulk insisted. "I lost my ring. This ring. I'm so glad you found it."

"That's not your ring," Trini said, glaring at him. "Now give it back."

"Sure it is." Bulk saw no reason not to get a free ring; especially one that was made out of gold and had a fancy yellow stone.

Kimberly crossed her arms. "So if that's your ring, where did you lose it?"

"Well . . ." Bulk stalled for time while he tried to think. "I've been so many places today that I'm not really sure . . ."

"Where did you get it?" Trini asked.

"It's a . . . it was my grandmother's," Bulk told her, feigning confidence.

"No it's not." Kimberly tried to make a grab for the ring, but Bulk tossed it in a high arc over to Skull.

"Milk shake order, coming through," Ernie said, balancing five frothy milk shakes on a tray. "Will someone please close the shades? Gosh the light's bright in here," he said, trying to shade his eyes from the glare with one hand and keep the order balanced with the other.

In the blink of an eye, the milk shakes vanished. One second they were there on the tray and the next second they were gone. "Where'd they go?" Ernie asked, doing a double take. "What happened to the milk shakes?" Ernie rubbed his eyes, convinced he was seeing things.

"Give me that!" Trini said, snatching the ring away from Skull. "It's not nice to try to take things that don't belong to you."

Bulk wanted the ring and he wasn't afraid to deploy a little muscle to get his way, but just then he happened to catch a glimpse of Principal Strickland walking past the window.

He didn't want to take a chance that Strickland might come inside. So instead he just shrugged. "You can't blame me for trying."

Kimberly narrowed her eyes and glared at him. "Why can't I?"

"Hmm," Trini said, noticing that the brilliant yellow stone in the ring had turned to black. "That's odd." She tapped at the stone and then gave the top of the ring a twist. The stone turned back to its original brilliant yellow.

Ernie was still searching for the five missing milk shakes and growing more confused by the second.

He even went so far as to examine the underside of his serving tray, as if the shakes could somehow have gotten stuck down there. But he happened to do so just at the exact time that Trini twisted the ring. The milk shakes reappeared, but with Ernie inspecting the wrong side of the tray, they ended up dumping all over Bulk and Skull's heads.

"Hey," Ernie said, growing instantly annoyed. Bulk and Skull were always trying to cause trouble. "Stop horsing around, you two. You have to pay for those." He yanked the bill for the milk shakes off his pad and stuck it to Bulk's sticky forehead.

Kimberly and Trini hurried back to their table, nimbly leaping over the spilled shakes. "Did you see that?" Trini asked, after they'd taken their seats. "There's more to this ring than meets the eye."

"How so?" Billy asked, putting on his glasses to have a closer look.

"Well, after the milk shakes disappeared, the stone turned black," Trini explained. "Then I tried tapping at it and jiggling it around a bit. After that, I managed to twist the top and the stone turned yellow again."

"Yeah," Kimberly added. "And that's when the milk shakes reappeared."

"Interesting," said Billy.

"Cool," said Zack. "Let's give it a try."

"No, wait." Billy put out a hand to stop Zack before he could take hold of the ring.

"Hey," Zack said, mildly annoyed. "I'm the one who found it. I can look at it if I want to."

"I know," Billy told him. "But if that trinket is more than just a ring, then we don't know what it can do. I need to take it back to my garage and run a few tests in a controlled environment. We wouldn't want anyone accidentally getting hurt."

"I suppose you're right," Zack had to agree. "But if you're going to your lab, then I'm coming with you. I want to know what's going on with this ring."

"I wonder if it has anything to do with why Baboo and Squatt were at the cove," Kimberly said, thinking it over.

"It's got to be somehow connected," Jason agreed. "Tell you what," he addressed the group. "Why don't Kimberly, Trini, and I go back to the cove and look for clues as to how the ring got there and if it has anything to do with Rita. Zack will go with Billy to his garage to run some tests and try to figure out how the ring works."

Everyone was in agreement. Zack nodded. "Sounds like a plan."

Chapter 9

"Whoa!" Squatt wailed, crashing into his friend as they landed back at Ria's fortress on the moon. Having fled Earth in such haste to get away from the Power Rangers, their return was a bit rough. It was a little embarrassing, but neither one of them was particularly known for bravery.

"Ouch!" Baboo cried after being knocked over by his klutzy friend. "Watch where you're going, you clumsy oaf!"

"Sorry, sorry, sorry," Squatt apologized, rolling off his fellow minion. Grabbing Baboo by the arm, he tried to yank his friend to his feet.

"Where's Rita?" Squatt wanted to know, glancing around. She was usually in her observation room, squinting through her telescope at Earth, and at Angel Grove in particular.

"I don't hear her charming voice." Baboo looked

around the empty observatory, as well. "She must be somewhere with Scorpina. After all, they are old friends, you know."

The half warthog–half blueberry thought it over, rubbing his enormous blue chin. "Wouldn't it be funny if they were braiding each other's hair?"

Baboo took a swat at his fellow minion, but missed. "Don't say things like that!" he snapped, causing Squatt to giggle.

Then, from somewhere deeper in Rita's lair, angry voices could be heard. "How could you have lost it?! How could you have lost the Eclipse Ring? You only had it for five minutes and now it's gone?!" Rita didn't believe in hiding her emotions. "This is exactly like the last time, when we were conquering the Xelton Galaxy!"

"Zelton Galaxy!" Scorpina shouted back. "And that was not my fault. You try keeping ahold of jewelry while fighting a multi-eyed, gassy swamp monster. I needed one hand free just to plug my nose."

Rita wasn't backing down. "You could have tried using the ring on the swamp monster. Did that ever occur to you?" she bellowed.

Scorpina wasn't backing down, either. "That was completely not my fault, and you know it!"

"Well," said Squatt, rubbing his ears to stop them from ringing. "They're here. I guess we'd better tell Rita and Scorpina that we know what happened to the ring." He started to head toward the door to search for their overlord.

"Wait," said Baboo, catching up to him and putting a hand on his shoulder. "What if we didn't?"

"Didn't what?" Squatt asked. He was never the first to catch on. "What do you mean?"

"Well . . ." Baboo adjusted his monocle. "If we tell Rita that the Power Rangers found Scorpina's ring, what do you think will happen?"

"Well . . ." Squatt repeated, thinking it over. "Rita will probably order Scorpina to get it back."

"That's right." Baboo nodded. "And how do you think she'll get it back?"

Squatt squinted his tiny eyes and rubbed his giant blue chin; he didn't have a good brain for answering questions. "Um . . . I guess she'll go down to Earth and maybe fight the Power Rangers to get it back."

"And who do you think Rita will want to send with

Scorpina to fight the Power Rangers?" Baboo asked.

This really threw the big blue warthog. "Uh . . ."

"Us!" Baboo hissed. "You and me. Rita will demand that we go with Scorpina down to Earth. And you know the Power Rangers aren't going to just hand the ring over."

"Yeah," Squatt agreed. That's pretty much how he imagined things would go.

"And then Scorpina will probably want to fight the Power Rangers," Baboo pointed out.

"I bet she will," his blue friend agreed. "For someone so cute, she can be kind of cranky."

"And she'll expect us to fight with her," Baboo replied. "And if we don't do everything exactly the way she wants, we'd better watch out." He pantomimed a scorpion's tail with his arm and pretended to sting.

"Oh!" Startled, Squatt jumped back, his eyes wide with fright. "I don't want that. I don't want to do any of that."

Baboo nodded vigorously. "So why don't we simply tell Scorpina that we don't know what happened to her ring?"

"Yeah, but we do." Squatt still wasn't clear on the whole plan.

"But we can pretend like we don't," Baboo pointed out. "And I can offer to make her a new one. A better one. One with more jewels."

"One that can fly!" Squatt added, still confused, but getting caught up in the excitement.

"No, not one that can fly, you nitwit." Sometimes Baboo found his friend to be quite frustrating. "But as far as Rita and Scorpina are concerned, we don't know anything about who found the ring."

"Who found the ring?!" Rita demanded as she came sweeping into the room, her long staff in one hand and her robes trailing behind her.

"Where is it? Who has it?" Scorpina demanded, entering the room hard on Rita's heels. "Just name a name and I'll make them regret the day they tried to steal from me," she said, running a hand over the handle of her gold, crescent-shaped sword.

"What ring?" Squatt said. "We don't know anything about a ring."

"He means we don't know where the ring is, Your Majesties," Baboo said, quickly giving his friend a sharp elbow.

Rita glowered at them. "Now, why do I get the feeling that you're not telling me the truth?" Her free hand tightened into a fist. "And if I did find out you were lying, then I don't even want to think of how angry I would be," she snarled, banging the bottom of her long wand on the marble floor and causing the fortress to rumble with the echo.

Baboo's knees instantly started to tremble. "I mean that we don't know where it is at this exact moment," he insisted, completely abandoning his plan. "But we did happen to see one of the Power Rangers find it while they were playing their weird game."

"The Power Rangers have my ring?!!!" Scorpina shouted so loud that it probably even hurt her own ears. "Where are they? I will crush them into sand!"

"Well, it's funny you should mention sand, your scorpion-ness," Squatt said, "because—"

"Because the Power Rangers found your ring on the beach," Baboo said, cutting off his friend so that he could be the one to share the news. "They found it almost exactly where we landed."

"And you birdbrains didn't take it back?" Rita

demanded, practically shouting in their faces.

"We tried," the minion insisted. "We sent the Putties, but the Power Rangers managed to fight them off."

"You sent the Putties?" Rita said disdainfully. "Leave it to the two of you to avoid getting your hands a little dirty by sending in the Putties."

"But, your evilness, there was nothing we could do," Baboo insisted.

Squatt was quick to add, "The Power Rangers are very powerful fighters. I mean, they've even got the word *power* in their name."

"Did they use their Zords?" Scorpina wanted to know. She had her arms crossed and she was glaring at the minions in a very disdainful way.

"Well . . . n-not exactly," Baboo stammered. "But, I mean, they easily could have. And there's nothing the two of us could have done against their Dinozords."

"You two imbeciles disgust me!" Rita raged. "You let the Power Rangers get ahold of the Eclipse Ring with only a Putty fight?" She shook her fist in the air. "I should banish you to the bowels of the galaxy for such a show of cowardice."

"But, your exalted overlord," Squatt protested. "Don't you always say that Earth is the bowels of the galaxy?"

This caught Rita off guard. After chewing back some of her fury, she admitted, "I do say that from time to time, don't I? Then you two wastes of space will go with Scorpina, find the Power Rangers, and get the Eclipse Ring back!"

"I don't want to be burdened with these two idiots," Scorpina insisted, shaking her head. "It'll be easier to conquer the Power Rangers without these goofballs getting in my way."

"But we know where they are right now," Baboo said, suddenly eager to join Scorpina.

"We do?" Squatt asked him in a quiet aside. This surprised him. "Aren't we trying not to go back down to Earth?"

In a whisper, Baboo asked, "Would you rather stay here with Rita right now?"

Squatt's eyes bulged a little at the thought of staying with the sorceress when she was in such a foul mood. "Yes, we definitely know where they are," he insisted to Rita. "Scorpina," he added, "we can lead you right to them. The Power Rangers are as good as yours."

"Fine," Scorpina said, relenting with an irritated sigh. "But don't get in my way or you'll taste my crescent blade."

Chapter 10

Zack was bored. He was with Billy in the garage and he couldn't find anything to do. At first he tried helping his friend, but the Blue Ranger's brain was wired completely differently than most human brains, and Zack—as well as the other members of the team—frequently found it very challenging to keep up. Trini could sometimes tune in to Billy's wavelength, but Zack, Kimberly, and Jason usually didn't have a clue.

The great thing about Billy, Zack mused, was that, even though he was a super-brainiac genius, he was also a really cool guy. Plus, he was a good fighter and an awesome member of the team. This was important because the Power Rangers all really counted on one another when it came to battling Rita and whatever destructive monsters she sent down to try to conquer Earth. That was never going to happen, as long as Zack and the other Power Rangers had something to say about it.

Once Zack began to realize that he was mostly getting in the way rather than helping, he tried working on some fighting techniques. The Black Ranger wanted to perfect his uppercut back kick and see how he could incorporate it with blocking techniques to make him a better fighter. Focusing on improving his martial arts skills was always a great way to pass the time. But after he'd executed a few of his more vigorous moves, Billy said, "Zack, that's looking good, but you're making me a little nervous. Some of my experiments are in a very fragile state, and I'm worried something might get damaged."

"I'll be careful," Zack assured him.

"I know," Billy said, "but that last kick came awfully close to my Power Crystal Dinozord enhancer. It's very delicate, and I haven't figured out how to make another one if this one gets destroyed."

"What is it?" Zack asked, looking at the multicolored crystal. "It's for our Dinozords?"

"Sort of. As you know, our Power Crystals are composed of our morphing essence," Billy began.

"Sure," Zack replied. At least he was pretty sure he knew what the Blue Ranger was talking about.

"Well, whenever I've studied any of our Dinozords, I've been gathering every bit of dust that I find from using our Power Crystals."

"Dust from our crystals?" Zack asked. "I've never seen any dust."

"It's microscopic," Billy assured him. "And there's not much of it. That's why this experiment has been so challenging."

Zack peered more closely at the rainbow crystal. "What is it?"

"I'm working on fabricating a Power Crystal that combines each of our Dinozord's strengths."

"Oh wow," Zack exclaimed. That sounded pretty good to him. "So we could all get one of these rainbow thingies and then we'd all be more . . . versatile with our fighting skills?" he asked, for lack of a better word.

"That's what I hope to do; but there's hardly any dust, so this is the only crystal I've been able to create so far, and it's very unstable." Billy shook his head. "I believe this one will work, but I'm not sure I can make another one."

"Oh. Got it." The Black Ranger backed away from the workbench. "No kicking around the rainbow Power Crystal. Not a problem." He had a ton of respect for Billy and his lab, so he knew to follow the rules. Plus, if Billy was too stressed worrying about his other inventions, he wouldn't be able to focus on the ring, and Zack was really curious about that intriguing trinket.

So then Zack thought he could work on some smooth dance moves, as long as it was nothing too energetic. He decided that might be a good way to pass the time. And that soaked up a few minutes, but it was hard to get in some solid practice when there was no music.

"Hey, Billy," Zack said, breaking Billy's concentration. "Sorry to interrupt, but why don't you have some music piped in here?" And then he offered, "I could set it up for you. It'd be easy."

"No thanks," Billy replied, "but I appreciate the offer."

"Why not?" Zack wanted to know. Setting up an awesome sound system for Billy would be an enjoyable way to pass the time. "I heard that listening to classical music while studying can help people to concentrate and absorb more information."

"True," the Blue Ranger said. "I've read a couple of those studies, but whenever I've tried, it never works for me."

"Why not?" Classical wasn't Zack's favorite type of music, but there was some interesting stuff and a lot of it was very pretty. *Besides*, Zack thought, *classical would be better than silence.*

Billy looked up from the ring and thought about it for a moment. "Because let's say I'm working and I've put on some Bach."

"Okay . . ." Zack said.

"Well, the more I listen, the more portions of my brain start to focus on the music," Billy said, setting down the powerful magnifying glass he'd been using to examine the ring. "Suddenly I find myself just thinking about Bach's motivic organization and his judicious use of counterpoint. And then I start thinking about how Bach was a musical pioneer of the Baroque period. And then I start to think about the influence he had over the composers of the classical period, most importantly Mozart.

And then suddenly I realize that whatever piece I was listening to is over and I haven't gotten any other work done."

"Wow," Zack said, staring at his friend, both amused and amazed. "I usually just want to know if the song has a good beat and if I can dance to it."

"So, anyway, that's why I don't want to have music in here," Billy said, picking up his magnifying glass and a pair of very small tweezers. "But thanks for offering."

"I think maybe I'll just lift weights for a while," the Black Ranger said. He needed to expel some energy and he was obviously distracting Billy even more than Bach. "Or do you need me for something?"

"Not at the moment," Billy murmured. He was already back to being deeply absorbed in how the ring functioned.

"Why do you even have weights in here?" Zack couldn't help but wonder aloud.

"I don't know," Billy said, not bothering to look up. "I think they were left by the previous—Hmm . . ."

"Hmm . . . what?" Zack asked, quickly setting the weights down and hurrying over to his friend.

"Hmm . . . bad? Or hmm . . . good?"

"Hmm . . . I'm not sure," the Blue Ranger admitted, scratching his chin. "But I think I know what this ring does."

"What?" Zack asked excitedly. He'd never been so curious about a piece of jewelry before, unless it was a championship ring for one of his favorite teams.

"Well . . ." Billy lifted up his glasses and rubbed the bridge of his nose. "You know how I've been doing work on molecular particle rearrangement?" he asked. When his friend didn't answer immediately, Billy added, "You know how I was telling you earlier about my work with the orange banana?"

"Sure," Zack said. That he remembered. Just the thought of it made him crave one of Ernie's strawberry-banana smoothies.

"Well, as far as I can tell, this ring appears to operate on the same principal. But instead of rearranging molecules, it seems to . . ." Billy searched for the right word.

"What?" Zack asked, completely fascinated. He wasn't quite sure where Billy was headed with the whole thing, but he really wanted to know.

"Um . . ." Billy furrowed his brow. "It . . . it seems to erase them."

"Erase them?" Zack's eyes widened as his gaze shifted over to the ring. "Erase them how?"

"I'm not sure yet," Billy said, frowning at the trinket. "I need to run some more tests on this erasure ring."

"So it's an erasure ring?" the Black Ranger asked, reaching out to touch the piece of jewelry.

"Best not to do that," Billy said, blocking his friend's hand. "I don't know the ring's full capabilities."

"Oh, come on," Zack said. "Can't we just erase one little thing? It just sounds so cool."

Billy pinched his lips together. "Well . . ."

"We could make the weights disappear," Zack suggested, trying to think of something that his friend wouldn't value.

"Better keep those," Billy said, "for when you and Jason are over."

"True," Zack said with laugh. "But can't we erase something else? I mean, something small," he added. "Please?"

"Well . . ." Billy thought it over some more. "I do happen to have a lot of extra bananas around right now, so I suppose we could test it, as long as it's in a controlled environment."

"Yessss!" Zack said, breaking into a huge grin. Testing stuff was the fun part of science as far as he was concerned.

A few minutes later, they had everything set up. Billy had improvised a small stand for the ring, and they'd put a banana on a plate. "I think we should clear everything out of this corner of the garage before we try anything," the Blue Ranger said. "I wouldn't want to make the lawnmower disappear; my parents would think I was trying to get out of mowing the lawn."

"No problem," Zack said, rushing to clear the corner. He couldn't wait to see the erasure ring in action.

Once the corner contained only the banana and the plate, Billy decided they needed protective eyewear. For a split second, Zack considered debating this with him, but then changed his mind. Billy was the science guy; he knew what he was doing. And if Billy said they should wear eye protection, then Zack was going to go along with it.

"All right," the Blue Ranger said, once they were

standing behind the ring. "See that tiny latch there?" He gestured with the tweezers. "I want you to lift it and then twist the gold jewel to the right."

"Why me?" Zack asked, suddenly wondering if testing the ring was such a great idea.

"Because you're the one with the sudden interest in science," Billy pointed out, giving the Black Ranger a playful nudge.

"Fair enough," Zack said. "I'll do it." Gingerly, he lifted the ring's tiny latch. "Okay, here we go." Reaching forward, he gave the top of the ring a twist to the right.

Instantly, a golden beam of light shot out of the ring, encompassing the banana and making it glow. A second later, the beam vanished and the fruit was gone.

Chapter 11

"This is where we set up the volleyball net," Trini said, surveying the ground of the cove. There were two depressions in the sand about thirty feet away from each other. "We put the poles there and there," she said, pointing to the depressions.

"That's right," said Kimberly, crossing the sand. "So when Zack dove to save the point, he must have landed about here," she said pointing to a spot on the ground.

Because of the battle, there were lots of tracks and marks all over the small beach that was part of the cove. There were several depressions in the sand that looked like they might have been made by a Power Ranger diving to save a point, but they could have just as easily been made by a sprawling Putty.

"Okay," Jason said, walking over to where the Pink Ranger was standing. "I know it's a long shot, but do you see anything?"

They all bent over, sifting their fingers through the sand. "This would be easier," Trini mused, "if we knew what we were looking for."

"I guess just anything that's out of place," Kimberly said. "Like the petals of a silk flower," she added, holding up a few scraps of lilac-colored material.

"Why did Baboo and Squatt try to send a Putty over to us that was dressed like a lady who gets a senior discount at the movies?" Jason wondered aloud.

Trini chewed on her lower lip. "That's right. Before the Putties attacked, there was that one all dressed up. Rita's minions must have sent it down to interact with us for some reason."

"That had to have been about the ring," Jason said.

Kimberly shrugged. "It's the only thing I can think of. But who of Rita's monsters would want a piece of jewelry, and why?"

The ground trembled slightly, causing the teens to brace themselves for something more dramatic. "Well, Trini," Jason said. "I guess we're about to find out."

Putty Patrollers appeared at the top of the bluffs, at least two dozen of them. "Putties," the Yellow Ranger said, although they all obviously saw them. "Okay, this should be fun."

"Should we morph?" Kimberly asked.

"No," Jason said. "Let's see what they want." The Putties stood at the crest of the bluffs, staring down at them, waiting for their next command.

"Maybe we've got them all wrong," Kimberly said as the three teens prepared for a fight, their backs to the ocean. "Maybe the cove is just where Putty Patrollers hang out when they're off duty, or something."

Trini pointed toward the top of the bluffs. "They brought Baboo and Squatt with them." The two minions immediately ducked down, although they were still easily visible.

"What are they doing here?" Kimberly couldn't help but wonder. "It's got to be about the ring. But who wants it? And why?"

"Maybe we should morph," Trini said. "You know they're not just here to surf. This has got to be one of Rita's sinister plans; we just don't know what it is yet."

Kimberly laughed. "And I doubt those two are

going to tell us. But I wish we knew who was behind their little visit."

"Look out!" Jason said, suddenly shoving Kimberly so hard that it sent her staggering.

"What?" Kimberly looked around, confused. "Where?"

"There," the Red Ranger said, pointing at a spot on the ground just inches from where she'd been standing; there was a black scorpion crawling across the sand.

Kimberly made a face. "There are no scorpions in Angel Grove. This can't be good."

"The last time I saw one of those," Trini added, backing up a few steps, "was when we were fighting—"

Seemingly from out of nowhere, a beautiful young woman dressed in gold armor like a scorpion shell appeared at the top of the bluff.

"Scorpina!" the three teens said simultaneously, with Jason pointing at their foe.

"What's she doing here?" Trini wanted to know.

"How is she even back here?" Kimberly added.

"I guess Rita called her back up to the major leagues," said Jason, eyeing the terrain. It was obvious they were headed for a fight.

Baboo and Squatt walked over to stand behind their royal scorpioness. "They aren't the one who found it," Baboo whispered in her ear. "It was Zack, the Black Ranger; he found your Eclipse Ring."

Scorpina's face transformed into a very charming and gleeful grin. "That doesn't mean they don't know where it is." After pretending to think it over for a moment she added, "Of course they might need some persuading before they'll tell me." Her left hand, the one encrusted in gold metallic plates, snapped menacingly.

"What are you doing back here on Earth?" Jason called to her. "What do you want, Scorpina?"

"I simply want what is mine," she called down to them, her tone cool and pleasant.

"And what's that?" the Red Ranger said, folding his arms and defiantly staring back at the gold-clad beauty.

"Hand it over without a fuss, and I promise I will destroy Earth quickly so no one has to suffer," the scorpion lady said, her voice as pleasant as the purring of a kitten.

"Hand what over?" Jason asked, feigning ignorance.

"My Eclipse Ring, you little—" Scorpina did her best to suppress her emotions, her deadly temper beginning to bleed through her calm appearance.

While Scorpina was distracted by speaking with Jason, Kimberly took the opportunity to tap at her wrist communicator. "Come in, Alpha 5. This is the Pink Ranger. We've got a major emergency. Over."

"What is it, Kimberly?" the robotic voice of Alpha could be heard to say after only a few seconds' delay.

"We're at the cove, and guess who else is here?" Kimberly said in a low voice.

"Who?" Alpha asked.

"Scorpina," Kimberly said, well aware of the weight that name brought with it.

"Scorpina is at the beach? Aye-yi-yi! That can't be good," the robot went on. "What is she doing there?"

"Besides trying to carry out Rita's plans to rule the Earth?" Kimberly said. "She lost a piece of jewelry and she wants it back."

The robot was quick on the uptake. "The ring that the Black Ranger found?"

"You got it," Kimberly said with a nod.

"Have you morphed yet?" Alpha wanted to know.

"Not yet," Kimberly told him. "But I have a feeling we're about to. And it's just Trini, Jason, and I. Zack and Billy are at Billy's garage."

"I'll contact them right away," the robot assured her.

"Thanks, Alpha," Kimberly said. "Pink Ranger out." With a tap of a button on her communicator she ended the call.

Chapter 12

"I see only three of you," Scorpina said, looking over the little group of teens. "Not your usual five. That means you won't be able to form the Megazord," she said with a small laugh. "This should be too easy of a victory."

"You should never underestimate a Power Ranger," Jason told her. Then, turning to his two friends, he said, "Come on, team. Let's do this. It's Morphin Time!"

"Right!" Trini and Kimberly both shouted.

Kimberly raised her Power Morpher to the sky and shouted, "Pterodactyl!" She then immediately morphed into the Pink Ranger, complete with pink helmet and suit.

Trini held her Power Morpher up to the sky and called out, "Sabertooth Tiger!" to become the Yellow Ranger.

"Tyrannosaurus!" Jason yelled, holding his Power Morpher to the sky. He instantly became the Red Ranger.

They managed to morph not a minute too soon because the Putties were already swarming down the bluffs toward them, ready to fight.

"Let's kick some Putty butt!" the Red Ranger said, striking a horse stance, his legs wide apart, one arm curved above his helmet, two fingers extended.

"We're with you," said the Pink Ranger as she assumed a bow stance, with one leg thrust behind her and the opposite arm in front, which brought to mind the fluid motion of an archer drawing back on her weapon.

"Let's show Scorpina what makes us tick," Trini said as she positioned herself in a resting stance. With her legs curled beneath her, she looked deceptively relaxed for someone who was about to unleash a mighty flurry of blows.

The Putties came plunging down the bluffs, and the battle began. "*Yah!*" cried the Red Ranger, somersaulting through the air and knocking down two Putty Patrollers with knife blade strikes.

"*Hi-yah!*" shouted Trini, spiraling through the air to meet a Putty head-on halfway down the bluff, knocking it down and seeing the creature tumble, felling two of its buddies.

"*Yeah!*" the Pink Ranger cheered, flipping over one Putty as it took a swing at her and seeing it sock one of its friends by mistake.

Scorpina appeared in their midst, clenching her metal claw and prepared to fight. "Where is the Black Ranger?" she demanded, scoring a body blow to the Red Ranger's solar plexus. "I've had enough of you nasty teenagers and your thieving ways."

"A Power Ranger would never steal," Jason informed her, managing to block her next strike and land a good flying back kick of his own. "We found the ring and we were trying to find its owner to return it before you showed up."

"*Gah!*" Scorpina bellowed. "Hearing what a bunch of do-gooders you are is even worse than when I thought you were trying to steal it from me." She drew her crescent sword. "I can't wait to be rid of you once and for all."

"I guess you'll have to learn to live with

disappointment," the Red Ranger said, doing a backflip to avoid the curved blade as Scorpina sliced it through the air, mere inches from the red fabric of his uniform. "Because we're not going anywhere."

"*Hi-yah!*" the Pink Ranger cried and leaped into the air, propelling her body, feetfirst, toward Scorpina.

"Too slow," the evil one said, narrowly dodging the blow. "You're no match for me."

"That's what you think," Kimberly informed her.

Scorpina began rapidly slicing at the air, forcing the Pink Ranger to do a series of backflips to avoid being cut to ribbons.

"Scorpina," the Yellow Ranger said, doing a leg sweep to knock over a Putty before turning to help her friend. "Why don't you go find another planet? Earth is taken."

But the evil scorpion lady managed to grab Trini with her enormous armored claw and then flung her across the sand. "Don't even begin to think you can stand up to me, you snot-nosed little twerps!" She obviously did not appreciate lively banter during a battle.

Six Putties managed to grab ahold of the Red

Ranger and launch him into the air. Jason was barely able to tuck himself into a ball so he could roll out when landing. A bit of breath was knocked out of him, but he forced himself to spring back onto his feet. "Come on, team, we need Dinozord power now!"

"Sabertooth Tiger Dinozord power!" Trini shouted, and her yellow Dinozord appeared as if sprinting out of the jungle.

Kimberly joined her, summoning her flying Dinozord from its volcano by calling out, "Pterodactyl Dinozord power!"

"Tyrannosaurus Dinozord power!" Jason called, causing his Dinozord to rise from the molten core of the earth.

Scorpina tilted her head back and released an amused laugh. "I can't deny that you're brave, Power Rangers, but without your Megazord, you don't stand a chance!"

Chapter 13

Meanwhile Zack and Billy were having a great time in the garage, using the ring to make things disappear. They'd already erased six strawberries, a cracker, a pile of leaves, a broken trowel, and a half-eaten sandwich that had gone stale.

"This is so awesome," Zack said, looking eagerly around the garage for more items to zap. "What else can we erase?"

"I'm reluctant to continue playing with the ring," Billy told him, even though he was enjoying himself.

"Why?" Zack looked disappointed. "This ring is a blast. I didn't know jewelry could be so fun."

"It is fun," Billy agreed, "but I don't fully understand how the erasure ring functions, so that makes it more dangerous. Plus, I have no idea where these items are going. Are they disintegrating? Are they in an alternate dimension? Are they being transported somewhere, reappearing in a garage in Alaska? Or on a tugboat in Bangkok? I have yet to figure it out." The Blue Ranger shook his head. "No matter how much I'm enjoying making things disappear with you, I think it's wiser if I continue with my analysis of the ring to identify the source of its power and fully understand how it works. We need to know the ring's potential."

The Black Ranger looked like he wanted to protest, but then he changed his mind. "Yeah, all right," he agreed. "You keep working on it, Billy. I should check in with Zordon and the rest of the team, anyway. I wonder if there's any news."

But before Zack had a chance to follow up on his words, his wrist communicator emitted six melodic beeps in a specific sequence. "It's the Command Center," he said to Billy before answering the call. "Zordon, it's Zack. What's happening?" he said into the device. "Did you figure out who is looking for this crazy ring and why?"

"Yes," came Zordon's deep, booming voice. He was an incredibly intelligent being from a distant galaxy who had been fighting Rita and her kind for centuries. But he'd been caught in a time warp and only appeared to the Power Rangers as a kind of blurry, floating head in a large glass cylinder housed at the Command Center, where he was tended to by his loyal robot, Alpha 5.

Zordon's low, distinctive voice always came out a little distorted as he straddled the space-time continuum. "The ring belongs to Scorpina," Zordon explained. "She has returned to Earth in quest of its return, and to finally achieve world domination for her old friend Rita Repulsa."

"Scorpina?!" the Black Ranger exclaimed. That was a name he'd hoped never to hear again.

Billy looked up from his examination of the fascinating piece of jewelry.

"This is Scorpina's?" he asked. Knitting his eyebrows together and giving the ring a closer look, he added, "Curious. What led you to that conclusion, Zordon? I see no markings of the scorpion in the ring's design."

"It was a gift from Rita. An exact copy of a ring that Scorpina lost during a battle many centuries ago," Zordon explained.

"Why would Rita give Scorpina a ring?" Billy wanted to know.

"Yeah," Zack added. "Rita doesn't seem like the gift-giving type of sorceress. At least not without getting something in return."

"Aye-yi-yi!" Alpha 5's robotic voice interrupted their conversation. He was unable to hold back his anxiety any longer. "Rangers, there's no time to waste. Scorpina's at Angel Grove Cove right now."

"The cove?" Billy frowned even more. "That's where the rest of the team were headed, looking for clues about the owner of the ring."

"That's why we contacted you, Blue Ranger," Alpha informed him. "Jason, Trini, and Kimberly are in trouble. Scorpina has a bunch of Putties with her, and your teammates already had to call upon their Dinozords to fight them off. I don't know how much longer they can hold out without your help."

Zack and Billy exchanged concerned looks. "Scorpina's all kinds of trouble," Zack said. "We need to get to the cove and fast."

"We should morph first," Billy said with a nod of his head as he quickly shut down some of the equipment he'd been using to examine Scorpina's little trinket. "We don't want any bystanders to recognize us."

"Definitely not," Zack agreed. A Power Ranger's secret identity as an average teenager was key to survival, and one of the crucial rules to being a Power Ranger. "Good idea. And let's take the ring with us," he said, picking it up. "We might need it. We can erase Scorpina from the history books."

It was obvious from the expression on Billy's face that he wasn't thrilled with the idea. "I don't think that's a good plan, Zack. We only have a basic understanding of the ring; we only have an elementary idea of its capabilities. We know how to make things disappear, but we haven't figured out how to bring them back. Why would we risk it?"

"We know it can erase Scorpina off the map. That's good enough for me," Zack insisted. But when Billy still appeared reluctant, the Black Ranger added, "Don't you remember the last time we fought Scorpina? It was brutal. We almost didn't survive. I mean, any of us. And if we don't survive, then Earth doesn't survive. I'm not willing to take a chance on the whole planet going down. That's just not a risk I'm willing to take." He held Scorpina's ring firmly in his fist. "I say, we've got the weapon and if things get tough, then there's no reason we shouldn't use it."

The Blue Ranger still wasn't comfortable with deploying the ring, but his friend did have a good point. "Let's check in with Zordon first. He knows a lot more about this stuff than either one of us."

"If Scorpina's on the loose, we don't have a moment to lose," Zack insisted. "Let's just get to the cove. If we think we'll need to use the ring, then we'll give Zordon a quick buzz."

Billy reluctantly agreed. "Okay, but we have to be careful. We don't want to accidentally transport Scorpina into a shopping mall in Baltimore or something like that. We should only use it as a very last resort."

Zack pinched his lips together, but also nodded his head. "Okay," he agreed. "But if we use the ring as a first resort, then I think the battle will go a lot quicker."

This earned a laugh from Billy. "Are you ready to

morph so that we can teleport to the cove?"

"You bet I am. We need to help the other Rangers." Zack took ahold of his Power Morpher. "It's Morphin Time!" he said in a loud voice. "Mastodon!"

Billy followed suit, raising his Power Morpher in a steady grip and shouting, "Triceratops!"

No Power Ranger would ever stand idly by knowing that a teammate was in trouble. Moments later they were a black and a blue streak in the sky as they teleported to the cove.

Billy and Zack landed just in time to see their fellow Power Rangers leaping into the air to access their Dinozords. "Looks like we got here just in time," Billy noted.

"Why don't I treat Scorpina and the Putties to a blast of the erasure ring, and we all go out and grab a burger?" Zack suggested.

"Negative," Billy said. "Remember the mall in Baltimore? We can't take that chance unless things get really desperate."

"Fine. You're right," Zack said. "I'll just hold on to it while we make short work of Scorpina and friends." With that, he began patting down his Ranger suit.

"Hey. Have you ever noticed that our uniforms don't have any pockets?"

"Look out!" Billy shouted as a Putty Patroller lunged at the Black Ranger.

"*Yah!*" Zack shouted as he repelled his foe with a mighty spear-hand to the throat, which immediately took the wind out of the Putty's sails, dropping the creature to the ground.

From her lair on the moon, Rita Repulsa glared into her telescope. "Curses! It was going so well, and now the rest of those snot-nosed brats have shown up. I can't stand it when they do that!"

Finster, the ghostly owlish-looking creature that was Rita's chief monster maker and in charge of keeping a good supply of Putties at the ready, was at his sorceress's side. "We could send more of my Putties, most evil one. I have some piping hot from my monster machine."

"Putties," Rita grumbled with a disgusted snort. "I have a better idea."

Taking the long wand with the crescent moon on top that she always carried and holding it like a javelin, the sorceress raised her voice and shouted,

"Magic wand, make Scorpina grow!" And then she hurtled it toward Earth.

As the wand pierced the crust of Earth, the ground split and bolts of electricity flashed and danced, filling the air with sparks. A pulsating light encompassed Scorpina. She threw back her head and laughed, fully realizing what was coming next.

Scorpina began to grow at a rapid rate. Soon she was towering over the Power Rangers, as tall as a twenty-story building, her hulking mass throwing a shadow across the cove. And not only was she a giantess, but Scorpina had transformed from a coy and charming woman into a grotesque, mutated scorpion with mandibles extending from her jaws and an enormous claw strong enough to cut a Power Ranger in half.

"Wow!" said Zack, awed by the ginormous creature before him. "I always think my memory has exaggerated Scorpina's appearance into something much scarier, but it really hasn't."

"It's time for some dino-power," Billy said, deflecting a Putty with a shoulder roll and then following through to knock the creature to the ground.

"Let's join the others and call our Zords."

"Great idea," the Black Ranger said, before deploying his Power Morpher and shouting, "Mastodon Dinozord power!" His Dinozord appeared from a snowy tundra.

The Blue Ranger joined him. "Right behind you," he said. "Triceratops Dinozord power!" he shouted while raising his Power Morpher, causing his Dinozord to appear as if straight from the desert.

Zack wasn't quite sure what to do with the ring before accessing his Dinozord. He thought maybe he could tuck it into his belt somehow, but as he was quickly trying to figure something out, Scorpina lashed out with her tail, striking at him.

"You're the Ranger who stole my property!" Scorpina screeched. "Give it back to me!"

The Black Ranger was barely able to dive-roll out of the way, almost losing his grip on the ring.

"That was a close one," Billy called out to him as he was leaping into the air to access his Dinozord. "You okay, Zack?"

"Yeah, fine." The Black Ranger leaped back on his feet, as nimble as a cat. "Let's get in our Dinozords and—" His words petered out as he looked around for his friend. "Billy?" Zack spun around, trying to look everywhere at once, but seeing his friend nowhere. "Billy?!" he said again.

There was no reply.

Chapter 14

Scorpina slashed at Zack again, electricity shooting out of her tail's stinger. The Black Ranger managed to dodge the blow, two Putties getting zapped by the bolts of lightning in his place.

Zack scanned his surroundings again. Billy was nowhere to be seen. "Team," he said, contacting the others with his wrist communicator. "Can anyone see Billy? We were just about to access our Dinozords, but now I can't find him anywhere."

"I'm not seeing him," came a reply from the Red Ranger. "His Triceratops isn't moving. Get in your own Dinozord immediately. We can't fight a supersized Scorpina from the ground."

Leaping into the air, Zack entered the cockpit of his Mastodon. "I'm in," he updated the team. Glancing down at what he had clenched in his hand, he noticed something that made the bile rise in his throat. The stone on top of Scorpina's ring was black, indicating that it had recently been fired. Zack had accidentally deployed the erasure beam. "Oh, no," he said, feeling a cold ball of dread building in his belly. "I think I might have accidentally erased Billy with the ring."

"What?" Kimberly yelled from her Zord as she soared through the sky. "You couldn't have. But I can't see him anywhere." And then she tried using her communicator. "Billy, this is Kimberly. We need you to call in. Can you hear me? Billy, if you're out there, we need you to make contact right now."

They heard nothing but dead air.

"His Dinozord isn't moving," Kimberly said, flying past the Triceratops again. "I don't see him. I don't think he's in there."

Scorpina closed in on the Triceratops, wrapping her tail around it and shooting lightning bolts into the machine. The Dinozord trembled and shook.

"I hope Billy's not in there, or he'll be toast," Trini said before using her Sabertooth Tiger to shoot several laser blasts at the hideous scorpion monster that Scorpina had become. Even though most of the shots were a direct hit, the monster was unfazed.

"Zordon, Alpha 5, did you see what happened to Billy?" Jason asked, connecting with the Command Center. "He can't just be gone."

"Negative, Jason," Alpha 5 said.

"I'm afraid we don't see him, Rangers," Zordon said. "I'm afraid he has vanished."

"We need to form Megazord," the Red Ranger said.

"But how?" Trini wanted to know as Scorpina retaliated, lashing at her Sabertooth Tiger Dinozord with her deadly tail. "We need Billy, and he's simply vanished." The Blue Ranger's Triceratops faded back to the sand dunes from which it came.

"I should have never brought this stupid ring," Zack said, giving Scorpina an icy blast from his Mastodon's trunk. "Billy said I shouldn't bring it, and I wouldn't listen to him."

"Well, we need to figure out what happened to Billy, and fast," the Red Ranger said. "Everyone, get ready to teleport to the Command Center, immediately."

"But how?" Trini asked. "It's not like Scorpina's just going to let us teleport out of here. Not if she can help it."

Fortunately, at that exact moment, Scorpina's wildly thrashing tail crashed into a boulder, causing her to howl in pain. Seizing the opportunity while the monster was distracted, the Red Ranger shouted, "Alpha, we need to teleport now!"

"You got it!" said the robot. Moments later there were four colored blurs racing across the sky to the remote location of the Command Center up in the hills.

"Aye-yi-yi," Alpha 5 said as the Power Rangers arrived at the Command Center. "I only see four of you? This is very bad. What happened to Billy?"

"That's what we're here to find out," Jason said. The four of them were back to their regular appearances as average teenagers, no longer in their Power Ranger uniforms.

Hanging his head, Zack blurted, "I think I might have erased Billy with Scorpina's erasure ring."

"How could this be?" the robot asked, hurrying over to examine the ring that Zack was still clutching. "You don't usually have something like that happen with a piece of fine jewelry."

"It's the ring that I found at the beach. Billy

called it an erasure ring because it can make things disappear."

"Disappear like Billy," the Red Ranger said grimly.

"How does it erase things?" Alpha 5 wanted to know. "This ring needs closer analysis."

"Let's get to it," Trini said. "There's not a moment to lose."

Zack slumped into a chair, cupping his head in his hands. "This is my fault. Billy said not to bring the ring because he didn't fully understand how it works, but I wouldn't listen."

"Hey, hang in there," Jason said, patting his friend on the shoulder. "We need you focused so that we can get Billy back."

"If we can get him back," Zack mumbled miserably. He knew he had to fight past his feelings of guilt so that he could focus on helping. "Zordon," he said, looking up. "What do you think? Where's Billy? Do you have any idea?"

Zordon, who had been unusually quiet since the Rangers' arrival, then spoke, his voice booming. "I am still able to detect the Blue Ranger's life force on the beach that you call the cove, even though he is not visible to the human eye."

"So, what do you mean?" Zack walked over to stand directly in front of the clear cylinder where Zordon's disembodied head appeared as a giant, wavering image. "He's, like, invisible?"

"Not exactly," Zordon replied. "All I know so far is that, even though the Blue Ranger is not physically at the cove, some aspect of his life force is still present."

"So then we can get Billy back?" Kimberly asked, walking over to stand by Zack's side.

"That is unclear," Zordon told her. "But I think there must be a chance."

"A chance. That's not great," Zack said, shaking his head.

Kimberly gave his hand a squeeze. "Come on, Zack. It's better than no chance."

"Rangers," Zordon said rather suddenly. "I'm sensing a new threat at the Angel Grove Mall."

"Sensing?" Trini asked. Zordon usually had a clear view of any of Rita's flunkies that showed up on Earth.

"I don't have a visual yet," Zordon explained. "But a large crowd has gathered in the parking lot of the

Angel Grove Mall, and it seems to have something to do with Goldar."

"Goldar!" the Rangers all exclaimed. He was one of Rita's most powerful fighters and he'd teleported to Earth before, to fight side-by-side with Scorpina.

"He's obviously here to help Scorpina, but why is he at the mall?" Zack asked.

"That is currently unknown. But we must protect the Angel Grove population," Zordon said.

"Plus protect the cove. Plus find a way to get Billy back," Kimberly pointed out. "How are we going to cover all of that?"

"I'll go to the cove," Jason said, "to keep an eye on Scorpina. Zack and Kimberly, you need to go see what Goldar is up to. And, Trini, you should stay here and try to figure out the ring with Alpha 5 and Zordon."

"No," Zack told him. "You go with Kimberly. I'm the one who needs to face Scorpina."

The Red Ranger shook his head. "I know you feel responsible for Billy's disappearance, but we're a team. And with a villain like Scorpina, you know it's going to be an ugly fight."

Zack thought about it for a moment before saying,

"No, it has to be me. I need to own this. And besides, I think I have a way to get an edge over that golden lobster; at least for a little while."

"What is it?" Trini asked. All of the friends were eager to know.

Zack actually managed a smile. "Just another little mad-scientist project that our friend Billy's been cooking up in his garage."

Chapter 15

Zack didn't like to have to go into Billy's garage when he wasn't home, but seeing that the continued existence of the planet depended on Zack being able to keep Scorpina at bay until the rest of the team figured out a way to get Billy back from wherever he'd gone, Zack figured Billy wouldn't mind.

"Hmm," Zack said, rubbing his lip as he stood in the middle of all of Billy's experiments.

Where was that crazy rainbow crystal thingy that Billy had somehow managed to make? Zack scanned Billy's numerous workbenches. He knew that he'd been practicing his uppercut back kick when Billy had asked him to stop.

The Black Ranger oriented himself in the garage so he was facing the same direction that he had been earlier in the day. But he just didn't see the crystal anywhere. Zack remembered that Billy had swiftly cleaned up a few things before they'd left to help the team at the cove. He'd probably tucked the Power Crystal away somewhere to keep it safe.

Zack began quickly and carefully rifling through the wide variety of inventions and equipment. He didn't want to damage anything, but he also desperately needed something to give him an edge— even a temporary one—while battling the giant scorpion monster. Billy's experimental Power Crystal was his only chance.

"*Gah!*" Zack exclaimed, feeling frustrated, yet trying to treat all the fragile equipment with care. "Where is it?!"

His hands found a bundle of flannel wrapped around something hard. "Please, please, please," the Black Ranger whispered under his breath. "Yes!" He'd found it.

Billy's prototype rainbow Power Crystal was there. It had all five colors: red, black, pink, yellow, and blue. Zack had no idea how Billy managed to create half the things he did, but he desperately hoped that the Power Crystal would work.

Raising his Power Morpher to the sky, Zack called

out, "Mastodon!" and immediately transformed into the Black Ranger. Once fully disguised, he activated the teleportation mode on his wrist communicator, remarking to himself, "It's time to hit the beach."

Chapter 16

Seconds later, Zack was jetting across the sky at such an accelerated speed that he was nothing but a black blur as he headed to Angel Grove Cove. And not a moment too soon. Scorpina was furious that the Power Rangers had teleported off the beach while she'd been distracted. Her plan had been to lure the teenagers back to the beach so she could finish them off. But how, she wondered, angrily thrashing her deadly tail back and forth with irritation. She needed to smash some buildings or something; that usually brought the Power Rangers running.

"Uh . . . excuse me, your royal scorpion lady," Squatt called up to the giantess. He and Baboo had been hiding high up on the bluffs, out of harm's way during the battle, but he had noticed Zack landing on the beach in his Power Rangers uniform. At first he wasn't going to say anything, but then he thought it could be something that the scary scorpion lady might like to know.

"What is it, you blue toad?" demanded Scorpina.

Squatt was insulted, but he thought it probably wasn't the right time to point out that he was more closely related to a warthog than a toad. "Well, I just thought you'd like to know that the Black Ranger is back," he said. "And he's the one who found the ring in the first place."

Scorpina moved her giant monster head back and forth trying to fix her gaze on Zack. He looked so small and vulnerable, standing defiantly on the beach like a mouse confronting an NBA player. "Hey, Scorpina," he shouted. "How about picking on someone nowhere near your size?"

The scorpion giantess thought that sounded like a great idea. Raising her great tail, she lashed out at the Black Ranger, causing the hero to somersault into the air. It was only Zack's lightning-fast reflexes that saved him from a potentially deadly blow. Missing her target caused Scorpina to scream with rage and frustration.

"Whoa," Zack said to himself. "I'd better get into my Dinozord, and fast. And hope this Power Crystal does what I hope it does." Then, in a steady voice, he called out, "Mastodon Dinozord power," causing his Dinozord to appear as if just emerging from a snow-covered tundra.

"All right!" Zack whooped as he launched into the air to enter his Dinozord.

A split second after he'd engaged the Mastodon's controls, Scorpina struck again, this time wrapping her tail around the Dinozord and giving Zack a zap of electricity that made his teeth rattle.

"Cool off!" Zack shouted, triggering his Mastodon's trunk, covering Scorpina with a heavy blast of snow and ice. That loosened the monster's grip a little, and gave the Black Ranger the space he needed to deploy his secret weapon.

"It's crystal time!" Zack said. Taking a deep breath, he inserted Billy's rainbow Power Crystal into the slot on his Mastodon's control panel, murmuring, "Here goes nothing."

The first hint that Billy's attempt to combine the essence of all the Rangers' powers into one crystal was a success was immediate, as a sparkling rainbow glow filled the control room of the Dinozord and then spread over the Mastodon's entire body.

"Cool," Zack marveled as he felt the power of Jason's Tyrannosaurus, the grace of Kimberly's Pterodactyl, the intelligence of Billy's Triceratops, and the fearlessness of Trini's Sabertooth Tiger coursing through his Zord.

Scorpina also recognized that something had changed; she took a hesitant step backward, releasing the Mastodon for a moment as she assessed the new situation.

"Hey, lady," Zack said from inside the cockpit of the Dinozord. "Time for you to learn to play nice."

The scorpion monster had another idea in mind. She raised her giant claw and struck at the Black Ranger's Dinozord. But with the Yellow Ranger's added agility, Zack was able to dodge the blow. "Awesome!" Zack said, pumping his fist in the air, amazed at how easily he had avoided being hit. "It's working!"

Normally the Mastodon Zord didn't have access to a variety of lasers, but with Billy's special crystal heightening his power, Zack was able to shoot Pterodactyl-power lasers from his Zord's eyes, giving Scorpina a good jolt. "I am loving this mega crystal-power!" Zack said. "I hope it lasts." The multicolored glow enveloping the Mastodon hadn't faded yet, fueling the Black Ranger's confidence.

"Let's try a little wrestling of my own," the Black Ranger said, manipulating the Mastodon controls so that the robot's trunk wrapped around Scorpina, pinning her arms to her sides. With the added strength of the Red Ranger's Tyrannosaurus strength, he was able to keep his grip while both freezing her with arctic snow and giving her another laser blast.

Scorpina shrieked and thrashed wildly, but it took several seconds before she was able to break free from the Mastodon's grip. Staggering backward, the scorpion creature released an angry cry and tried to clamp Zack's Dinozord in her giant claw.

"No, thank you," the Black Ranger said, using his Dinozord's trunk to thrust the claw away. But it wasn't as easy this time. Zack couldn't feel the full strength of the Tyrannosaurus coursing through his Zord. He still felt stronger, but just not as strong as he had when he'd first inserted the crystal.

Glancing at the rainbow Power Crystal, Zack

thought that maybe it wasn't quite as brilliantly colored as it had been at Billy's place. "Sure hope the team doesn't take too long to find Billy," the Black Ranger said to himself. "I have a feeling this special crystal isn't going to last forever."

Chapter 17

Meanwhile, back at the Command Center, Trini, Alpha, and Zordon were hard at work. "Okay, Alpha," Trini said. "Is the test object in place?"

"Ready and waiting, Yellow Ranger," the robot said, in an almost chipper voice. He loved helping the team, even if he was worried about Billy.

Trini looked over her shoulder at the robot. He had placed a pair of pliers so they would be in line with a beam from the ring. "Good," she said. "Let me know when you're clear." The Yellow Ranger was glad Alpha wanted to help find Billy, but she didn't want to accidentally send him to join Billy.

Alpha 5 distanced himself several feet from the pliers. "Clear," he said.

"Test firing Scorpina's ring, third attempt," Trini said, lifting the latch and twisting the stone on top. As soon as she did, a golden beam shot out of the ring and surrounded the pliers, making them glow. Seconds later, the tool was gone.

"The stone's black again," Trini said, examining the ring once the beam had ceased.

Alpha hurried over and stared at the spot where the pliers had just been. "It's possible that they disintegrated, even though I see no evidence of it."

Trini took a moment to consider that depressing possibility. "No," she said, shaking her head. "Zordon said he could feel Billy's presence still on the beach. He can't have dis—" She didn't want to finish her thought. "There has to be a way we can get him back. I mean, we got the milk shakes back at the Youth Center, right? So there's got to be a way."

"Trini and Alpha." Zordon's voice suddenly boomed to life. "Have you discovered the secrets of Scorpina's ring?"

"We've discovered half of it," Trini said ruefully. "Making things disappear is the easy part. Getting them back is a lot more challenging."

"Zordon, how are things going for Zack?" Alpha wanted to know.

"And are you still able to detect Billy?" Trini added.

"I can still detect the Blue Ranger at the cove," Zordon told them, "and Zack has been holding his own with Scorpina."

"That's a relief," said Trini.

"But," Zordon added, "I don't know how much longer the Black Ranger can hold out. He's been using a special Power Crystal that Billy was working on, but it is only a prototype and is very unstable. I fear the added strength it was giving him has started to dissipate. Look into the viewing globe to see for yourselves."

Trini and Alpha gazed at a large, clear globe in the middle of the Command Center. It was about the size of a big-screen TV. Zordon could use the globe to show images from other places on Earth. The team saw Zack's Mastodon as it battled the supersize Scorpina. The Dinozord had a sparkly multicolored light all around it, showing all the colors of the Power Rangers, but the light wasn't steady; it was flickering in and out.

Just then Scorpina lashed out at the Black Ranger with her tail, sending sparks flying. They could hear the air crackle with electricity. The Mastodon managed to avoid most of the strike, but the tip of the tail scraped along its metal hide, leaving a burning trail.

"I need to teleport over there," Trini said. "Two Zords are better than one."

"Negative," Zordon told her. "The Black Ranger can hold out for a little longer. You must focus on the ring and finding Billy. Only by forming Megazord will Scorpina be defeated."

"Well, what about Kimberly and Jason?" Trini asked, adjusting the rubber band she was using to tie back her hair. "Is Goldar at the mall?"

Chapter 18

By the time Zordon had teleported Kimberly and Jason to the Angel Grove Mall, a crowd had already gathered around a large red-and-white structure that had been erected in the center of the parking lot.

"That looks like a stage," Kimberly said, squinting as she peered across the sea of cars. "Maybe Goldar is switching careers to something in entertainment."

The Red Ranger shook his head and gave a rueful chuckle. "Come on," he said, starting to jog toward the crowd. "Keep your eyes open for trouble."

As the Rangers got closer, it became obvious that the large group of people really were standing in front of a temporary stage. No one was performing yet, but there were workers on the raised platform doing sound checks.

"I don't see Goldar anywhere," Jason remarked after scanning the crowd. "What is going on?"

"Look." Kimberly pointed. "There's the Archer twins. They'll know what's happening." She raised her voice and called, "Lexi! August!"

Two teenagers looked around to see who was trying to get their attention. "Hey, it's Kimberly and Jason," Lexi said, pushing her wavy blond hair out of her bright blue eyes. "Hi!"

Her twin, August, whose eyes were the same color blue, but who wore his sandy brown hair cut short, smiled and gave a friendly wave. "What's up?" he called. "Are you Goldstar fans, too?"

"Goldar's here?" Jason asked, checking the crowd again, his muscles tensed for a fight. But everyone seemed calm and reasonably happy. "Where?"

"They haven't started yet," August told him.

"Wait. What?" Kimberly was confused. "Did you just say Goldar or Goldstar?"

"Goldstar," Lexi said with a laugh. "You know, the band."

"They are performing here," August added. "You're lucky you got here in time because they're going to start any minute."

Lexi cocked her head to one side. "Did you know

that? Or are we giving you the news?"

"It's news to us," Jason said, smiling with relief.

"We had no idea," Kimberly admitted.

"That's okay. You can hang with us," August told them. "We love this band; it's going to be great."

"Oh, um . . ." Kimberly stammered. "We need to do some shopping. It's kind of an emergency birthday present situation. But we'll try to catch up with you later."

"Okay," Lexi said. "We'll be here. We're not missing Goldstar for anything."

"Come on, Kimberly," Jason said with a tug on her sleeve. "We've got to go."

"See you later," August said with another wave.

Just then, a woman up onstage approached one of the microphones. "Ladies and gentlemen, I give you Goldstar!" A group of men and women clad in elaborate, sparkly gold costumes rushed onto the stage and started playing their first song.

"We need to call in to the Command Center," Jason said, "but I think it's too loud."

Kimberly shook her head and pointed at her ear. "I can't hear you; it's too loud."

"Let's get to the car," Jason said, gesturing in the general direction of where they had parked.

"You can tell me in the car," Kimberly shouted back. "Once we're away from Goldstar."

Chapter 19

Back at the Command Center, Trini was pondering the ring. "I just thought of something," she said. "You know at the Youth Center with the milk shakes? Right before they reappeared, I had the ring," she told Alpha and Zordon. "I twisted the top of the ring back to the way it had been. And then Bulk and Skull got drenched with the shakes. At the time, everything was happening so quickly that I didn't know what was going on, but now I'm thinking differently. I had to have done something to make the shakes reappear."

"But we've tried turning the ring the other way," Alpha pointed out. "The stone turns back to yellow, but it doesn't do anything else."

"I know." Trini nodded her head. "But we've only tried it in a controlled environment; I wasn't holding the ring. You know, really gripping it." When Alpha 5 cocked his big metal head to one side, she added,

"I mean, maybe by squeezing it, I somehow activated it, or pressed something, or . . . I don't know . . ."

"Maybe it was the heat from your hand," Alpha 5 suggested.

"Maybe." Trini thought it over. "But I wasn't holding it for that long."

"Let's try to reenact the scene at the Youth Center," Alpha said. "We keep making things disappear in a controlled environment, but maybe we need to get a little more hands-on."

The Yellow Ranger shrugged. "It's not the scientific way, but I'm up for anything at this point."

"Alpha began clearing equipment off of a table. "We've got to get this ring thing figured out."

"You know what?" Trini said, scratching her head. "I really didn't think about it earlier, but Scorpina called it an Eclipse Ring. At least that's what I think she called it."

"Aye-yi-yi," the robot said, putting both hands on his metal head. "An Eclipse Ring makes sense."

Trini's eyebrows rose high on her forehead. "How does that make sense?"

Alpha thought about it for a moment. "With an

eclipse, it seems like something has disappeared, but it's really still there."

"That's true." Trini nodded. "It's an optical illusion."

"So if it's an Eclipse Ring, then Billy must somehow be concealed, but he's still really there," Zordon said excitedly. "Trini, try to remember how you were holding the ring when the milk shakes dumped on Bulk and Skull."

The Yellow Ranger walked over and tentatively picked up the ring, careful to keep it pointed away from Alpha and Zordon. "Okay, let's see," she said, thinking hard, trying to remember. "The stone was black, like it is now. And I was trying to keep it away from Bulk and Skull, so I was holding it like this." Trini demonstrated, gripping the ring between her thumb and forefinger. "And I had my hand kind of wrapped around it like this." She made a fist, with only the ring's stone peeking out the one end. "I was tapping at the stone, trying to figure out why it changed color. And then I twisted the top. But I was also squeezing the ring pretty firmly; I remember that." She closed her eyes and just felt the ring in her hand for a moment.

When she opened her eyes again, she looked under her thumb at the ring's design. "I think there's a little button here," she said.

Alpha hurried over. "A hidden button has got to do something," he noted. "Otherwise, why have one?"

"Try the ring. We don't have a moment to lose," Zordon said. "Zack cannot hold out for much longer, and I haven't heard from Jason and Kimberly about Goldar."

"Okay, stand back," Trini said. "Here goes nothing." With that, the Yellow Ranger gripped the ring firmly, allowing her thumb to press the button, and then gave the top a twist. A smoke-colored beam shot out of the ring, illuminating a silhouette of the pliers. And then suddenly they were back, along with a fuse and a burnt-out lightbulb, which were the other things they had made disappear in earlier tests.

"It's working!" shouted Trini, doing her best not to hop up and down because she was still holding the ring.

"Hooray!" Alpha 5 said. "Now we can get Billy back."

"We can get Billy back?" Jason asked as he and

Kimberly rushed into the room.

"Yes," Trini told them. "We've discovered the secrets of the ring."

"Jason, Kimberly, what do you have to report about Goldar making an appearance at the Angel Grove Mall?" Zordon asked, his voice filled with urgency.

"It wasn't Goldar at the mall," Kimberly explained. "It was Goldstar. They're a band, and they were doing a free show. You must have somehow picked up something about them."

"That's a relief," said Alpha 5.

"And now we can use the ring to bring Billy back," Kimberly said with a broad smile.

Trini frowned while studying the ring. "We really should run a few more tests first."

"No time," Zordon's voice boomed. "The Black Ranger needs your help now. Examine the viewing globe."

They rushed over to see an image of the Mastodon's cockpit. The multicolored light had faded to almost nothing, and the crystal the Black Ranger had been using to give his Dinozord some extra juice was starting to smoke. The image flickered, and then the viewing globe went dark.

"Zack," Kimberly said into her communicator. "Come in. We've figured out the ring and we're coming to help you. Over."

There was no response.

"Black Ranger? This is Pink Ranger. We've discovered the secrets of the ring and we're on our way to the cove to help you out and get Billy back. Over."

More dead air.

Kimberly turned to Zordon. "What's going on? Is he all right?"

"I am unsure," Zordon admitted, sounding concerned. "I cannot get a read on the Black Ranger."

"We have to get over there now," Jason said. "Everyone, are you ready to morph?"

"You bet we are," Trini told him.

Jason held his Power Morpher up to the sky and shouted, "Tyrannosaurus!" A moment later he was in his Red Ranger suit.

Kimberly did the same, shouting, "Pterodactyl!" She instantly became the embodiment of the Pink Ranger.

Trini also lifted her Power Morpher. "Sabertooth Tiger!" She instantly morphed into her yellow-clad alter ego.

Seconds later, there were three colored streaks racing across the sky headed for Angel Grove Cove.

Chapter 20

Zack was not having a good time in the cockpit of his Mastodon. The crystal was no longer giving off a multicolored glow. In fact, it was actually starting to smoke, and the air in the cockpit was becoming thick and making him cough.

"Think I'd better bail on this technology," the Black Ranger said, yanking out the crystal, which instantly crumbled into a million charred pieces. "The last thing I need is a fire."

Now it was just him and his Mastodon battling Scorpina. The Black Ranger hoped he'd survive long enough for his friends to arrive. But it'd been quite a while, and he hadn't heard from any of them. That wasn't typical for the team. Zack hoped nothing had gone wrong at the Command Center.

Scorpina could sense something was different. She eyed the Dinozord with suspicion. The shimmering glow that had surrounded the Mastodon had disappeared, and the creature appeared to be getting weaker. Scorpina knew that it was time to strike. She coiled back her deadly tail like a whip right before it cracks.

"This is going to be so sweet," Scorpina crowed as she closed in on the Black Ranger. "If you'd only given me my ring back, I would have made this quick. But you refused to cooperate, and now you're going to suffer. And so will your entire planet, since your cowardly friends ran away."

The Black Ranger knew this was probably the end of the line, but he was determined to go down fighting. "Bring it, Scorpina!" he shouted. "Give me everything you've got!"

The scorpion creature lashed out with her tail. Without the enhanced agility from the Sabertooth Tiger, Zack's Mastodon couldn't dodge the strike. Wrapping the Mastodon in her tail, Scorpina let loose jolt after jolt of electricity. Zack's Dinozord began to violently shake.

"I think it's time for me to bail out," the Black Ranger said. He hated to abandon his Mastodon, but knew it was better for the world if he lived, so he could keep on fighting.

Leaping from the cockpit of his Dinozord, Zack plunged to the ground and did a rollout across the sand. By the time he sprang to his feet, the rest of the Power Rangers were standing in front of him.

"Hey, Zack. Good to see you," Jason said with some relief, slapping him on the shoulder.

"Nice of you to show up," the Black Ranger replied. Turning to the Pink and Yellow Rangers, he said, "Did you figure anything out? Can we get back Billy?"

"Yes," Trini told him. "At least we think so." She pulled the Eclipse Ring off her finger. "Look here," she said, pointing out the well-concealed button. "If you reset the stone from black to yellow without pressing the button, then nothing happens; you can only make more stuff disappear. But if the stone is black and you twist it back to yellow while pushing this button, then you can make things reappear."

"Okay, got it. But where is Billy now?" Zack wanted to know.

"No idea," Trini told him. "But why don't you point this wherever you had it pointed when he disappeared and see if you can bring him back?"

"Rangers, you must hurry," Zordon's voice instructed from their communicators, "before Scorpina has a chance to gather her strength."

In her fury, Scorpina was still electrocuting the empty Mastodon. Finally, she let the Dinozord go, and it slowly tilted to one side and then crashed to the ground. Zack couldn't help but flinch. It felt like he'd lost a friend.

"Don't worry about it," Jason told him. "Just get Billy back."

"What are you going to do?" asked Zack.

"Call up our Dinozords and cause a distraction," was the Red Ranger's reply.

"Got it." Zack started sprinting across the beach, clutching the ring.

"Tyrannosaurus Dinozord power!" the Red Ranger shouted, calling up his Dinozord from the molten lava of the earth's core.

"Pterodactyl Dinozord power!" Kimberly cried, summoning her Dinozord from an ancient volcano.

"Sabertooth Tiger Dinozord power!" Trini yelled, bringing her Dinozord from the primordial jungle.

Zack tried to orient himself exactly like he was when Billy had disappeared. It was difficult to remember, and there weren't a lot of landmarks on the beach. Plus, they'd been in the middle of fighting a bunch of Putties, so that had been absorbing most of his attention.

Adjusting the Eclipse Ring on his finger, Zack pointed it in the general direction where he thought Billy might have been when he vanished. "Here goes nothing," he said to himself before pressing the secret button and giving the top of the ring a twist. A dark beam came shooting out of the ring, outlining several human-size figures. "Yes!" the Black Ranger said, convinced one of them had to be the Blue Ranger.

Half a dozen Putties took shape and then tumbled to the ground. "Okay, that's cool," Zack mumbled to himself, suppressing his disappointment when his friend didn't appear. "But Billy was leaping into his Dinozord when he disappeared, so I guess I have to aim a little higher."

Raising the ring while still pressing the button, he swept the air with the beam. A silhouette appeared, frozen in place as it was leaping into the sky. "That's gotta be him!" Zack said, holding his arm steady.

A few seconds later, the Blue Ranger tumbled to the ground. "Billy!" Zack shouted, rushing over to him. "You're back!"

"Am I?" The Blue Ranger was feeling a little dazed. Cradling his head with his hands, he said, "That was not fun."

"Where were you?" Zack wanted to know, helping his friend to his feet. "Wait! Look out!" he said, dragging Billy out of the way of Scorpina's tail as she tangled with Jason's Tyrannosaurus.

"I'll have to tell you later," Billy said. "Right now I think we need to dino up."

"Um . . . yeah," Zack stammered. "I think my Mastodon might be out of commission."

"Really?" Billy was surprised; the Dinozords could handle a lot of damage. "Why's that?"

"Well, I used that crazy multicolored crystal thingy you were working on in the garage to give my Mastodon extra abilities so I could distract Scorpina while the others were trying to figure out how to bring you back. But then the crystal started to smoke, and my Dinozord got sluggish. I had to bail out."

Billy nodded, trying to take it all in and process everything as quickly as possible. "It probably just overheated. Our Dinozords weren't meant to handle that much power. Hopefully just letting your Mastodon cool off will solve the problem."

"I hope so," Zack said. "We couldn't form the Megazord without you. And now that you're back, we can't form it without me."

Billy gave him a rueful smile. "That's the double-edged sword of being on a team, I guess. But I bet we can find a way to work together to take this galactic arachnid down." When Zack gave him a confused look, Billy added, "Scorpions are part of the same family as spiders."

"Oh." Zack gave a nod. "That would explain why this one is so ugly."

"Time to call on a little dino-help," Billy said as he saw Kimberly fly past Scorpina, treating her to a laser blast. "Triceratops Dinozord power!" he shouted, and his faithful Triceratops appeared as if charging across the desert.

"I guess it doesn't hurt to try," Zack said. Then, raising his voice, he called, "Mastodon Dinozord power!" Much to the Black Ranger's surprise and relief, his Dinozord began struggling to its feet.

"All right!" the Blue Ranger cheered. "Now let's see about taking down this eight-legged freak!" With that, he launched into the air, accessing his Triceratops.

"Right behind you," Zack told him. "But first . . ." The Black Ranger started waving his arms, trying to get the scorpion monster's attention. "Scorpina! Hey, Scorpina!" he yelled. When she finally turned her head to look in his direction, Zack added, "Do you want your ring back?"

Scorpina took a step in the Black Ranger's direction, obviously eager to get back her possession. Zack cocked his arm. "Well then, go get it!" he shouted, throwing the ring as far as he could into the ocean, where it was immediately engulfed by the waves.

Chapter 21

"Nooooo!" Scorpina shrieked at such an earsplitting volume that all the windows on Angel Grove buildings facing the beach rattled.

The Black Ranger didn't pause to savor the moment. He was already sprinting for his Mastodon, and moments later he was launching into the air to access its controls. Much to Zack's relief, he found his Dinozord was in good working condition. Billy had been right about it just needing time to cool down.

"Who's ready for Megazord?" the Red Ranger asked, now that all of the Power Rangers were in control of their Dinozords and had communication access.

"I am!" shouted Kimberly as her Dinozord soared over the beach.

"Count me in!" said Billy, his head already clear and his body ready for action, even after his bizarre disappearance.

Trini chimed in with, "Now's good for me," as she deftly made a tight turn with her Sabertooth Tiger to take another pass at Scorpina.

"Happy to be part of the team," Zack said, relieved to have Billy back, but also pumped and ready for action.

"Okay then," Jason said. "We need Megazord power, now!"

Each Power Ranger felt the special energy and excitement that ran through their blood when forming Megazord. It was every member of the team coming together to create one amazing fighting force. Their Zords began converging, all racing in a precise formation until they became a single fighting unit. Trini and Billy formed the legs of Megazord, giving it stability during battle. Zack formed the two big laser blasters on the tank, giving the firepower necessary to subdue a foe like Scorpina. Jason formed the body of the tank with the strength of a Tyrannosaurus so that the assault vehicle could withstand a beating from almost any opponent. Kimberly finished off the Megazord with the ferocity of her Pterodactyl riding at the very top.

Even though each Power Ranger was in a separate part of the Megazord Tank, they were connected by the unifying power of the Megazord, which made it feel like they were all sharing the same cockpit.

"Everyone's fully engaged?" the Red Ranger asked.

"Yes!" said Zack and Billy, both giving a thumbs-up.

"Right!" said Trini and Kimberly, both pumping their fists in the air.

"Great," Jason said. "Now let's blast this crawdad back to the Stone Age!"

There was a blast of the Megazord cannons; a direct hit to Scorpina's chest. The giant scorpion beast staggered back a few steps, but then recovered and came straight at the tank, swinging her crescent sword and putting a tremendous dent into the hull.

"Ouch!" cried Trini. It was her portion of the tank that had taken the blow and she felt it personally.

"Wow!" The Blue Ranger was amazed. "That was both barrels, and Scorpina barely felt it."

"I think she's extra mad because I threw away her toy," Zack commented.

"That's what you get for tossing someone's jewelry," Kimberly informed him as she did a flyby, blasting Scorpina with her wing-mounted lasers.

"When will I ever learn?" Zack replied with a shake of his head.

Despite their joking around, the Power Rangers knew they were in deep trouble. If a full blast from the Megazord Tank cannons wasn't enough to slow Scorpina down, there was only one thing left to do.

"It's time for Megazord Battle Mode," the Red Ranger shouted. "Everyone get ready; we're going to Morph."

"You got it!" the Black Ranger cried.

"Ready when you are!" the Pink Ranger radioed in.

"I'm with you!" the Blue Ranger said.

"No time like the present," the Yellow Ranger chimed in.

"Okay, team!" the Red Ranger said, giving everyone only a split second to prepare. "Let's do it."

The Triceratops and Sabertooth Tiger began to rise, forming the legs of the massive human-shaped robot of Megazord Battle Mode. The Mastodon converted, forming the core and arms of the body, with the Tyrannosaurus transforming into the head. For the Megazord to be complete, the Pterodactyl joined in, forming the breastplate.

"Now we're ready to rumble," said the Red Ranger. "Come on, team, let's send this uninvited guest out of here in a galactic taxi."

Scorpina was one step ahead of the Rangers, attacking with a fierce swing of her sword. Megazord ducked the blow, spun around, and then executed a mighty roundhouse strike that sent the scorpion beast staggering.

Recovering quickly, Scorpina used her tail in a maneuver that was usually a classic leg sweep. Megazord leaped over the electric tail, but while dodging the blow, the robot got caught right inside Scorpina's giant, terrifying claw. And it clamped down tightly.

"*Ugh*, I can't move," Zack said. "She's got our arms pinned."

"Stomp on her foot," Jason commanded. "Anything to get us loose before she brings in the tail."

"On it!" Trini said, delivering a crushing blow to the top of their enemy's foot.

"*Gah!*" the Red Ranger said as the horrible scorpion claw began to slowly crush the metal chest cavity of

Megazord. "Rangers, ready your Power Crystals."

"Right!" the team shouted as a single fighting unit.

Scorpina's golden claw was tearing through Megazord's metal sides. The Power Rangers were seconds away from being cut in half.

"Ready!" the entire team shouted. Then, with Olympic-level precision, the Power Rangers inserted their Power Crystals into the slots on their Dinozords' control panels.

The Megazord was suddenly filled with a new strength and energy. A vicious head butt rang Scorpina's helmet, causing her to loosen her grip enough so that Megazord was able to get one arm free. That was all the opportunity the Rangers needed.

"Time for a little Power Sword!" the Red Ranger shouted.

A bolt of lightning raced across the sky, and then a sword as long as a school bus sped down from the heavens. Megazord easily caught the weapon and began hacking at the scorpion monster while fending off blows from her deadly tail.

"Yeah! Take that, you giant cockroach!" the Black Ranger yelled.

"You tell her, Zack," Billy chimed in.

Scorpina released an ear-shattering roar. She was furious, but also fully aware that she was about to be defeated. "You horrible, thieving peons!" she yelled. "I will destroy you! You will never be rid of me!"

But those were only idle threats; Scorpina was growing weaker. She managed to deflect another blow from the Power Sword with her immense claw, but it obviously took something out of her. Megazord did a spinning back kick and sent Scorpina stumbling.

"You'll never win," she said, staggering. "Rita will never stop until Earth is destroyed."

"That's never going to happen as long as the Power Rangers have anything to say about it," the Red Ranger told her.

After another blow from the Power Sword, Scorpina was finished; she had no fight left in her. Megazord raised its sword for a final blow, but Scorpina turned and ran. A moment later, she had teleported, making her escape.

. . .

Back on the moon, Rita was furious. "What are you doing back here?" she demanded, once she realized that Scorpina had given up the fight and fled back to the fortress.

"Just grabbing my stuff," Scorpina said. She had transformed back into a beautiful woman clad in gold armor. "I didn't want to forget my other boots," she said, hastily throwing a few possessions into her bag.

"The Power Rangers are still alive! Get back down there and fight!" the sorceress bellowed.

"Sorry, Rita. I just remembered something I've got to do," Scorpina called before she teleported out of the solar system. "Thanks again and sorry about the ring. I'll see you in a couple of centuries."

Chapter 22

"Wahoo!" the Power Rangers shouted, high-fiving one another as they jumped out of Megazord. As soon as they were all clear, the giant robot disassembled into the Dinozords, which went off to conceal themselves in their secret locations.

"I can't believe Scorpina ran away," Trini said, laughing. "That was too good."

"She left so fast, I guess she forgot to take her crew with her," Zack said, pointing to the crest of the bluff where Baboo and Squatt were still hiding.

"I say we get 'em!" Jason said, pretending like he was about to start chasing Rita's two minions.

"They see us!" Baboo squeaked.

"Let's get out of here!" Squatt added, but he was speaking to thin air because his friend had already taken off with all the Putties.

That gave all the Power Rangers a good laugh.

"I need to call in and update Zordon," Jason said, tapping at his wrist communicator. "Come in, Zordon and Alpha 5. Billy's back, and Scorpina has been sent packing."

"Congratulations, Power Rangers," Zordon boomed. "You continue to impress me with your fighting skills, loyalty, and teamwork."

The Power Rangers all smiled at one another. "Thanks, Zordon," Kimberly said. "We like you, too."

"You can give me a full report later, Power Rangers," Zordon said. "Right now, I think you deserve some time to celebrate your hard-won victory."

"Thanks, Zordon," Zack said. "It's nice to take a break from saving the world every once in a while."

"What do you say we celebrate with some milk shakes at the Youth Center?" Jason suggested.

"Sounds sweet," Zack agreed.

"Plus, I want to hear all about what happened to you, Billy," Trini added.

"And where it happened," Kimberly said. "You know, like what dimension."

"It's a shame about the ring, though," Billy said, shaking his head and gazing out at the ocean where the Black Ranger had flung it. "I didn't have time to fully understand the technology. That's something I really wish I could have done."

"Well . . ." Zack said, suppressing a grin. "Maybe you can."

"How?" Billy wanted to know. "I'll never be able to find it in all that water. Not in a hundred years."

"Maybe I didn't actually throw Scorpina's ring into the ocean," Zack told him. Then he pulled the Eclipse Ring out from where he'd hidden it in the cuff of his glove. "I might have thrown a rock instead. You know, just to fake out old lobster tail."

"Wow," Trini said, shaking her head. "Scorpina would never have left if she knew you still had that."

Her words made Billy frown and knit his eyebrows together. "Trini's got a point. No matter how much I want to study the ring, I think it would be better for the survival of the world if we destroyed it."

"Destroyed it?" Zack wasn't following his train of thought. "Why?"

"Because of Scorpina. We managed to defeat her this time, but it could have so easily gone the other way." The Blue Ranger shook his head. "No matter how much I want to keep the ring, I think we're better off if we destroy it."

The entire team thought this over. "You mean like go on a really long journey and then eventually end up throwing it into the mouth of an active volcano or something like that?" Kimberly asked. "Because that sounds a little epic-y."

"No." Billy had to laugh at the thought of the Power Rangers taking on the role of hobbits in a Lord of the Rings–style adventure. "I was thinking we could just melt it in my family's garage."

Everyone nodded their heads. "That sounds easier," the Pink Ranger admitted with a laugh.

Chapter 23

Talking about destroying the ring turned out to be a whole lot easier for Billy then actually destroying the ring. When they got to his family's house and headed into the garage, he put the ring in a crucible, but then he couldn't force himself to move forward from there. "It's just such a great piece of technology," he said. "I can't destroy it. Maybe if I just kept it for a little while and could study it very secretively and—"

"Sorry, Billy, it's just not a good idea," Jason said, lighting an acetylene torch and starting to heat the ring with the flame. "I don't want to stand in the way of science, but I also really don't want Scorpina coming back here anytime soon."

"I understand," Billy said, looking glum. "There's so much cool stuff in the world to study; I can't get hung up on this one thing."

"What do we do with it now?" Zack asked, looking

at the lump of hot metal once it had melted.

"I don't know," Jason said, using some tongs to dunk it into a bucket of water to cool it down. Then he reached in and pulled out the chunk of metal that used to be the Eclipse Ring. The stone had survived the heat and was imbedded in the blob. "It makes a pretty cool paperweight." Turning to Billy, he said, "Do you want it? You're the one who got erased into another dimension."

"No thanks." Billy shook his head. "Seeing it all the time would remind me of the technology we had to sacrifice."

"I'll take it if nobody else is interested," Zack said. "I think it would be something good for me to have around."

Just then the garage phone rang, and Billy picked it up. "Hello?"

"Helloooo," said someone using a weird-sounding, high-pitched voice. "I saw on a flyer that you found my ring. My sister and I are just so delighted because we've been worried about my ring. It was our grandmother's, you know."

"Oh . . . um . . . hold on a second." Billy covered the

mouthpiece of the phone. "I think it's Bulk pretending to be an old lady. He and Skull are trying to get the ring."

"You're kidding," Zack said, shaking his head. "Those two are—"

"Just tell them to get lost," Kimberly said. She was sick of those two lugs always causing problems.

"No, wait a minute," Jason said. "Maybe we can have a little fun with this. Tell them to meet you at Ernie's Juice Bar in the Angel Grove Youth Center and you'd be happy to return their ring."

Chapter 24

Forty-five minutes later, the Power Rangers were all dressed as normal teenagers, seated around a table at the Youth Center.

Ernie came over carrying a tray full of milk shakes. "Okay, let's see," he said, examining his order pad, "strawberry for Kimberly." He set a glass full of blended ice cream down in front of her. "Lemon chiffon for Trini . . . blueberry for Billy . . . cherry for Jason . . . and chocolate for Zack."

"Thanks, Ernie," the team said simultaneously.

"Hey, you guys all ordered what you're wearing," Ernie said with a broad grin. "You're matching."

"Huh?" The teenagers looked down at their clothes.

This made Ernie chuckle. "Trini's shake is yellow just like her shirt. Billy's shake is blue just like his overalls. It's the same for all of you."

"Well, look at that," Jason said, holding up his red shake to his red shirt. "It's almost like we planned it."

"Oh, oh. Quiet. I want to hear this," Ernie said, rushing over to turn up the volume on the television above the counter.

"This just in," a newscaster was saying. "Reports have come in that there was an attempt to destroy Earth by a giant scorpion creature from outer space. The alien was reported to have landed at Angel Grove Cove. Its plans to conquer Earth were thwarted by none other than our own local superheroes, the Power Rangers."

Everyone in the Youth Center began to clap and cheer.

"We'll have a better update as information keeps coming in, but I know I speak for all of us when I say that it's easier to sleep at night just knowing that the Power Rangers are out there, ready to protect us if necessary. Next up in the news, does your garbage disposal tend to sometimes smell like old food? It may be more sinister than you think . . ."

Ernie muted the television again and then let out a big sigh of relief. "I'd heard something was going on down at the beach today," he said. "I'm sure glad nobody was hurt."

"Us, too," Jason assured him.

"Thank goodness for the Power Rangers," Ernie went on as he gathered up some empty glasses to take back into the kitchen. "I hate to think of what would happen if they ever disappeared."

"Speaking of disappearing," Trini said, once Ernie was gone. "Tell us more about what happened, Billy. You said you felt like you'd been frozen for a moment, and then everything felt different, but exactly the same. How does that work?"

"It was very perplexing," Billy said, after taking a sip of his blueberry shake. "I could see all of you, but it was like there was a thick piece of glass between us. Everything was blurry, and I couldn't get your attention, no matter how hard I tried. I felt like I was a ghost or something."

"Sounds freaky," Jason said, wiping away a bit of a cherry milk shake mustache.

"It was disturbing," Billy admitted. "Plus, there were a bunch of Putties that got erased with me. And even though we were in an alternate dimension, their whole purpose is to attack Power Rangers, so that's what they kept trying to do."

"Sounds like you kept your wits about you," Kimberly observed.

"And used your fighting skills," Jason said, slapping the Blue Ranger on the back.

"I'm so sorry that happened, Billy," Zack said, hanging his head and unable to look in his friend's direction. "You told me we shouldn't bring the ring to battle Scorpina, but I wouldn't listen to you. And we almost lost you. That must have been scary being stuck in another dimension."

Billy patted him on the shoulder. "I'm okay. It was kind of scary, but everything turned out fine."

But Zack wasn't letting himself off the hook that easily. "I acted like an idiot. You're the scientific genius; you know your stuff. I should have listened to you. I'm just really glad you're okay."

"I appreciate you saying that, Zack," the Blue Ranger told him. "We all have our strengths and weaknesses. My strength just happens to be science."

"Just like how Zack can sometimes get a little dangerous on the dance floor," Kimberly said in a teasing voice, making everyone laugh.

"Speaking of dangerous," Zack said, looking across the room. "Whatever's going on over there can't be good."

Chapter 25

Everyone turned their heads to see two old ladies tottering into the Angel Grove Youth Center. The first lady was quite large, and almost as wide as she was tall, wearing a ridiculously tight skirt. The second lady was medium height and pretty thin, wearing a dress that fit like a circus tent. Neither one of them looked sweet or even very much like ladies. Even someone with bad eyesight could tell that it was obviously Bulk and Skull disguised as a couple of elderly women.

"Are they serious with those outfits?" Zack asked.

"Oh, excuse me," Bulk said, speaking in a high-pitched voice, but loud enough to draw the attention of the whole room.

"Sadly, I think they are serious," Trini replied, trying her best not to laugh.

"My sister and I are here to get our ring back," Bulk went on.

"Yes," Skull added in a high squeak. "It was our grandmother's, and we were so relieved to learn that some delightful teenagers had found it."

"Um, yeah. We found it. Over here," Jason said, waving at the two disguised bullies.

"Oh, hello there, young man," Bulk said, trotting over to their table in pointy-toed shoes that were too small and obviously pinched his feet. "Why bless your heart for finding our ring."

"It was nothing, ma'am," the Red Ranger said, playing along. "But just to make sure we're giving the ring back to the right people, would you please tell me what color stone is on the top?"

"Why, a yellow stone," the little-old-lady Bulk said with a lipstick-smeared smile.

"No, sister dear. It was a black stone," Skull corrected as he adjusted his hat so that it concealed more of his face.

"Which is it? Yellow or black?" Kimberly prodded.

"Black," said Bulk, accidentally smearing his lipstick even more across his chin.

"Yellow," said Skull, scrunching down under his hat in his attempt to not be recognized.

"Why don't you take a look at the ring and tell us if you recognize it?" Jason suggested. "I have it right here," he said, extending a folded-up napkin across the table. "We kept it nice and safe for you."

Bulk snatched the ring, and Skull made a grab for it a second later, knocking into his friend and causing him to drop the ring and the napkin. Bulk lunged for it, but his skirt was too tight and split straight up the back, revealing a pair of skintight boxer shorts with hearts and cupids printed all over them.

Skull spied the hole in his buddy's disguise. "B-Bulk!" he stammered, stepping behind the large teen to conceal his rear end. "Uh . . . I mean, Bulkatrice."

"Bulkatrice?" Kimberly wrinkled her nose.

Skull cleared his throat. "Beatrice. I meant to say Beatrice, but I have a bit of a tickle in my throat."

"What?" The disguised Bulk stood up, blissfully unaware that his skirt had split or that his accomplice was standing so close behind him.

Unfortunately, Skull wasn't expecting this move and he ended up getting clipped on the chin, sending him tumbling backward.

Bulk went to steady his friend by grabbing on to

his voluminous dress, but the fabric was so thin that it just tore instead, revealing Skull in a tank top and a pair of baggy white underpants.

"Oh my," Skull said, trying to cover everything at once. "Come on, Bulkatrice. If you have the ring, then let's get out of here."

Bulk checked the napkin. "Hey," he said, pulling out a plastic flower ring. "This isn't gold." He turned to confront Jason. "You're trying to steal our grandmother's ring."

"Oh, give it up, Bulk," Kimberly said. "We know it's you already."

"Fine," Bulk said, whipping off his hat as everybody in the Youth Center started to laugh. "So we wanted the ring. It's not like it's yours."

"Yeah," Skull added, wrapping the torn dress around his body like a toga. "Did you even try to find the real owner?"

The Power Rangers all exchanged knowing looks. Zack broke into a smile. "Let's just say that we took care of it. The ring is exactly where it's supposed to be."